ASH
A novel

Lisa Rowe Fraustino

•ORCHARD BOOKS•

NEW YORK

Copyright © 1995 by Lisa Rowe Fraustino

Orchard Books
95 Madison Avenue
New York, NY 10016

Manufactured in the United States of America
Book design by Rosanne Kakos-Main

10 9 8 7 6 5 4 3 2 1

The text of this book is set in 12 point Baker Signet.
The illustrations were done by Wes with a ballpoint.

Library of Congress Cataloging-in-Publication Data

Fraustino, Lisa Rowe.
    Ash: a novel / Lisa Rowe Fraustino.
        p.   cm.
    Summary: Eighteen-year-old Ash's change of behavior and its disruptive effects on his family are recounted by younger brother Wes.
    ISBN 0-531-06889-7.—ISBN 0-531-08739-5 (lib. bdg.)
    [1. Mental illness—Fiction. 2. Family problems—Fiction. 3. Brothers—Fiction.] I. Title.
PZ7.F8655As   1995
[Fic]—dc20   94-33008

For Dan,
the first Knight of Sisyphus,
who loves me like a rock
and pushes me back uphill
when I roll down

The Last Will and Testament of Wesley William Libby
age 15
(cause you never know when a truck's gonna hit you)

Being of sound mind and body, not counting pigeon toes and baby flab, I hereby declare this my 1st and last will and testament so far.

To my beloved mother Bonnie Lynn Tibbetts Libby I leave my Bible. But 1st my best friend Merle R. Daigle's gotta go through and erase some stuff. Merle, you know what I'm talking about.

To my beloved father Stefan Edward Libby, known to the rest of creation as Steve, I leave the violin you never wanted to buy me. Sell it and buy the CB you was always after us to pitch in and get you for Christmas. And if you dig deep into my closet you're gonna find an old G.I. Joe wearing them army medals of yours you LOST a few years ago. Don't get all mad that I didn't confess this when I was alive. You woulda killed me.

To my once-in-a-great-while beloved sister Deena T. Libby, OFFICIALLY known on her birth certificate as Dayna Theresa, which I personally think is a better name, I don't leave nothing.

No, just kidding Deena—you get the dust balls under my bed and the snotty handkerchief in my pants pocket when I die.

No, no, DEENA, just kidding! You can have my breadbox. Guess I should cross that out and write

1

"CD-radio," but Mama told me it was a breadbox under the Christmas tree and now that's what it is. Also, my entire CD collection, except for the Roy Boys Grammy Ethyl give me for my birthdays, and Grammy better take them back cause Deena would overreact if she had to share her room with Acuff, Rogers, Orbison & Clark.

To the aforementioned best friend Merle R. Daigle, who'd get embarrassed if I called him beloved so I won't, I leave my entire comic book collection except for the 1961 <u>Green Hornet</u> and the '62 <u>Wonder Woman</u> and the '65 <u>Superman</u> cause them's worth money and Mama & Daddy can sell them to pay for my funeral. Better clean out my college account at the Fleet Bank of Maine and use that for the funeral too. Only about $142.67 in there, so don't get no expensive casket. Cremate me. But that don't mean to keep my ashes around the house in no sicko urn. Bury them out back next to Togo, or put them in the cemetery with Grampy Libby. Even better, use them to fertilize Millard Worcester's blueberry field, which's got sentimental value to me but I can't say why cause it's Merle's secret too.

Merle also gets the personal effects in my locker if I die during the school year, but DON'T let NOBODY else in that locker, Merle, or I'll haunt you, I swear.

To the Cavalry Bible Church I leave all my clothes to put in a gar(b)age sale or give to the homeless cause Mama wouldn't have the heart to do it herself. Except my Knights of Sisyphus T-shirt—that goes back to Ash. The church can also have my baseball equipment, Scrabble, books and junk so the kids will finally have something to do when the parents are fellowshipping at covered dish suppers.

To my beloved brother Ashton Allen Libby I leave a composition book with some stuff written in it ONLY for him. Merle, you gotta get it for Ash out of the Shibboleth, and nobody else nag Merle to find out what the Shibboleth is cause that's just between him & me. Now Merle, don't get all mad, but the book's in a secret compartment that YOU don't know about. Take a hammer and pull up that floorboard with the big knothole, the one you always call Mrs. Fish-Lips' belly button. Then paw around in there till you find the book, but don't you dare read it or I'll haunt you <u>WITH CHAINS</u>, I swear. If it ain't there, that means I changed my mind and already give Ash the composition book.

If there's anything I left out then it ain't important and Deena can have it.

Just kidding! I didn't leave nothing out.

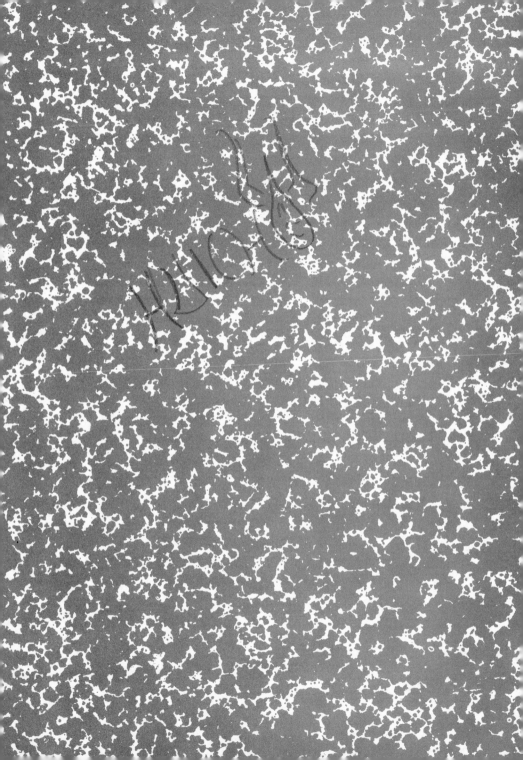

January 1

Ash—

Okay, I ain't much of a writer, but here goes my New Year's resolution. To write you how I seen what happened the last couple years.

The night we hit the moose was the beginning of you acting funny.

There's 3 types of Maine drivers. Molasses, whose foot sticks to the pedal at around 15 mph and whose tires stick in the middle of the road. Moderates, who drive normal—Mama's a Moderate. And Maine-iacs, who don't think nothing of cars coming in the opposite direction. A true Maine-iac will pass Molasses and Moderates anytime, anyplace, any weather. Never fails: a couple Moderates get stuck behind a Molasses going uphill around a corner in the rain, & before you know it a Maine-iac comes a-whaling by the lot of you. Maine-iacs are scariest when they're driving Mack trucks, or when they're your brother driving you home from violin lessons.

I tried to stop you. "C'mon Ash, since when was you a MAINE-IAC," I says. Nervous! I was white-knuckling the dashboard.

"Wes, Wes, Wes. Not to worry," you says, and give the engine another rev.

The speedometer thingy smacked bottom. KERPLINK, KERPLUNK, like the berries hitting the pail in that <u>Blueber-</u>

7

ries for Sal book you use to read me years ago. I known you all my life, 13 years at that time, and you never done nothing dangerous like that before. Maine-iac driving weren't like All-A's Ash. In-Good-with-the-Girls Ash. Star-of-the-Guitar Ash.

Remember when Daddy's VFW buddies heard you play at our 4th of July party the year you was 12? How they begged you to join their band? The Upcountry Boys was lousy at country & western, but they got popular around town cause you was so good. Especially for a little shit. Nobody ever called ME a little shit with admiration in their voice.

Rowboaters around here say they power their boats with "the ash breeze." Meaning ash-wood oars. You always made such a wake of excitement, when folks seen you coming they'd say, "Hold on to your hat—here comes THE ASH BREEZE!"

People even known me cause I was your little brother. At the Hancock Trading Post, at the Gull Rock Lobster Pound, at the Milbridge Cheap-O Cinema & especially at the RED BARN REDEMPTION CENTER, where bottles and cans get SAVED (har har), at all of these places it was always, "Hi-yah, Wes! How's Ash?"

When I was 6 I seen this guy on public TV playing a violin real flashy. Great jumping Scott, if I could play like that! Nobody could convince me that I couldn't just pick up the violin and make beautiful music rubbing them 2 dingahookies together.

"Once you start, you're sticking with it," Daddy says. Making out the check for my violin. Pre-owned by someone who didn't stick with it.

"Course I'm sticking with it. Like Ash," I says. Like a dummy. You picked up your guitar & made music while I hacked at the violin & made a mess of scales and TECHNIQUES with weird names like staccato and spiccato. Nothing ever come easy to me. It's like I got hand-me-down GENES, left over after you & Deena. Sun in your hair, ocean in your eyes. Me? Dried-out pine needle hair and mud eyes. You 2 never had to wear clothes from the Husky rack. You 2 never worn out the inside edge of your shoes.

I ain't got blue eyes and I ain't got perfect pitch, I hate playing violin and I'll never get the guts to quit after Mama & Daddy put out all that lesson money. This is one of the secrets why I don't want nobody reading this stuff but you, ASH.

Paying attention, Merle? CLOSE THE BOOK <u>NOW</u>.

Did that last page sound jealous? Wrong! The thing is, I WORSHIPPED you, Ash. You was easy to believe in. But it was hard to believe we was actually swaying 80-per all around the Milbridge Road.

"You pissed off or something?" I asked, since Grammy Ethyl weren't there with her mouth soap. Already known the answer, though. You didn't like having to drive 30 miles to the Pierre Monteux Music School for my violin lesson instead of jamming guitar with your friends. Mama & Daddy couldn't drive me. Had alot to do back home getting Libby's Motor Lodge & Campground ready for the season.

The instant our 2 right wheels rounded that corner by the road sign to the Unionville Church of God, I seen a giant black lump licking salt off the road. And I felt sick about what was gonna happen. There weren't even time to get braced or say a prayer. The brakes screamed panic-stricken as our bumper cut the legs out from under the moose. I went THUD against the windshield and woke up in a screaming ambulance. Which is why I can't give no grisly description of what a totalled moose looks like. But I can guess.

A Totalled Moose

You was in the ambulance too—a blood trickle drying on your forehead. "Wes, you okay, guy?"

I kinda grunted. Okay my foot. My head felt like a gigantic bruise. Which it was. I touched my forehead. Warm, oozy, raw.

"Bumped your noggin real good—you'll probably rent a room in the hospital a couple days," says the paramedic.

Then you felt bad. Real bad. I known cause you bawled harder than that colicky baby in Rm. I at the motor lodge the hottest night of August when I was 10. Since then the folks try to put babies down to the end in Rm. 10.

Mama & Daddy weren't too pleased to get the call from the hospital. It didn't help that Deena was giving them a hard time about sucking the winter gunk outa the pool. Afraid she'd get crud under her nails before her exciting youth group date with The Hormone, AKA Kenneth Pike. So when the phone rung, Mama & Daddy wasn't in the mood for an emergency.

The doctor made a joke about maybe putting Mama in the hospital for shock. She said something about maybe having to put Mr. Ashton Allen Libby in after Daddy got through with you. You told Daddy the natural consequences was punishment enough already.

I had what they called "concussion presenting w/ contusions & symptoms of vertigo." Actually, I ached. Everything was cotton balls around the edges. Had a few stitches & a dizzy headache for a few days. Grammy Ethyl come over and watched me a week straight for signs of brain damage. "Uh, don't you mean signs of NEW brain damage?" says the darling Deena.

The folks never did manage to get the pool ready the weekend of the accident. You had to fork over the money for car insurance, or else you couldn't drive the new (used) Blazer that replaced the one you staved all to hell. And that was the time we hit the moose.

Looking back, I realize that was the 1st time I noticed you weren't yourself. But I didn't think much about it at the time. Nobody did.

January 2

Spring was busy with stuff like Deena's idiotic junior prom. Before The Hormone & his mother come for her she waltzed into the living room on her tiptoes. "Don't I look like the <u>Nutcracker</u> Snow Queen in this dress?" she says.

"The Nutty Buddy at Dairy Queen, more like," says me.

Deena the Prom-Dairy Queen

PTHT!

12

Grammy Ethyl, who come over to capture that very moment, flashed her Polaroid just as Deena stuck her royal tongue out at me. The Queen garbage-disposed the picture. Too bad you missed it.

Whoops—skipped Easter.

Easter always brings in a crowd up to Cavalry Bible. Daddy use to make you & me run up there early to save a good pew in the back where Pastor Pudgy's stare couldn't reach. Excuse me—Pastor BRADLEY LOVELL. Daddy & Grammy Ethyl always call him Pudgy (even though he ain't no more) cause that was his nickname growing up. Daddy & Pudgy was like me & Merle, best friends all the way back to diapers. So chummy, they use to stop off for a beer every morning on the way home from 3rd shift at the blueberry cannery. Till Pudgy got born again and Daddy didn't. Which was the beginning of why Daddy took a backseat Easter Sunday.

Also, Daddy liked to sneak into church after Mrs. FISH-LIPS set down and get outa there before she stood up to leave. Mrs. PIKE, The Hormone's mother, get it? The woman considers it her Christian job to be everyone and their brother's keeper, and if the church ain't crowded, she gets a pew to herself cause nobody wants to be the brother next to her when Pastor calls sinners up front to repent and get saved. Her elbows get to going like fins, flapping you towards the Lord.

"How's that Steve Libby? Land a Goshen, I ain't seen him here since Christmas. Or was it EASTER?!" she use to always say whenever she could catch holt of Mama's elbow on the way in or out of church. "Almost forgot what he looks like."

HER husband has the only good excuse for missing church every Sunday—he met his maker. She herself skips one Sunday a year to go down to Portland for the state convention of the Women's Christian Temperance Union, where they know better than Bud Wiser. She comes back all gung ho and on a membership drive for teens who'll swear off hard cider and sex education.

If this was for Miss Small's writing class she'd call Mrs. Fish-Lips a FLAT CHARACTER and make me say something nice to round her out. There must be something—let me think. Okay, I once seen her in a tender moment with Kenneth. Holding a Kleenex so he could blow his nose.

Anyways, thanks to the concussion you give me, Mama let me stay home that Easter. After you'd left early for pew duty, and the folks had left with Deena at the last minute to avoid Mrs. Fish-Lips, I popped open some root beer & chips & turned on the TV to watch the immortal Wile E. Coyote. You all got home 1/2 an hour later than usual. Daddy went straight to the fridge and swigged 1/2 a bottle of Bud.

"Ashton," he says, "saving the front pew ain't funny."

You & Mama & Deena all looked at each other and laughed tears into your eyes. Too bad I missed the cause of that.

In May you graduated from Narraguagas High. Of which there's always a certain part of the student body bent on changing it to Narragansett High and the school logo to a 16-ounce beer can. The evenings you wasn't at a graduation-this or a graduation-that, you was at a graduation party.

"You know Ash is drinking his head off at them parties," Deena says one night at the supper table. We'd waited the chop suey an hour before we choked it down without you.

"If Ash can drink his head off," Deena says, "I don't see why I can't have a beer once & awhile."

Daddy's eyes opened all the way, then slitted like a venetian blind when you yank both strings to figure out the direction. "NegaTIVE. Ash is 18," he says, "he's going through a stage, and he's a boy."

"Whoopy ding. I'm 17, I'm going through a stage, and I'm a girl," says Deena. "You drink 2 beers everynight—you going through a stage too?" Maybe I don't got the whole thing right, but that's what Deena said word for word. You don't forget lines like that.

I chomped chop suey so I wouldn't laugh. Daddy don't like us kids laughing when he's making a point. There's a fine line between his sense of humor and his belt. Which he never uses but frequently unbuckles to show he's serious.

Daddy leaned into Deena's face. "Then let me put it another way. Ash is graduating from high school, he's becoming a man, and he can't get knocked up."

"In case you don't know, Daddy, beer drinking don't get you PREGNANT."

Deena's got a smart mouth on her. The one thing I gotta admire about her. When Daddy goes drill sergeant on me, all I can say is the first syllable of something numb.

"Deena! Steve! If we're going to carry on this kind of conversation, we should do it later on." Mama's eyebrows pointed right at my chin. Sign language for, "Don't talk like that in front of the baby." She knows I'm 15 now, but whenever she tucks me in it's still, "You'll always be my baby."

Daddy give Deena another 2 seconds of stare, then, "You're right, Bonnie. Wes, don't you got some dishes to clean up?"

I known he'd do that—it's his military training, 6 years of "Yes, SIR!" He's the drill sergeant, but Mama's the major. And Grammy's the 4-star General.

Me, I'm on KP.

January 3

The day before my spring concert I was on the toilet practicing my music and wishing you'd broke my bow arm instead of my head open in that accident, when you mosied in to prime up at the medicine cabinet mirror. "No wonder your teacher has you practicing in the bathroom. Your vibrato STINKS, Wes old boy. P-U!"

I weren't mad—you was right. Bathroom acoustics was suppose to improve my ear for music, but I known it was my fingers that stunk. After you left, I ditched the vibrato and practiced pure notes for 3 HOURS so you'd be proud of me at the concert. I always wanted to make you proud. More you than even Mama & Daddy & Grammy Ethyl. Maybe it's cause you was so good to me when I was little. Like the time me & Merle'd been in Millard Worcester's blueberry field. Which I weren't suppose to be anywheres near or Daddy said he'd teach me what it really means to unbuckle a belt. Usually I was pretty moderate about berry pigging, but that year I ate so much I was throwing up blue 1/2 the night. Daddy says, "You been into Millard's blueberries, ain't you, Wes," and started unbuckling.

You was in the bathroom door listening and says suddenly, "Wait, Daddy, it's my fault. I BOUGHT him a box of berries for helping me clean campsites. Didn't I tell you not to eat your pay all in one place, Wes old boy?" You looked at me hard, like you was sending a silent message, "Keep it shut."

I grunted an ayuh.

But that was nothing compared to the time you saved me & Merle's life. We was just 4 or 5. When the memory comes back it ain't full of tastes, smells or fingertip feelings like other memories. More like a movie. Something I watched instead of lived.

Merle & me are playing beside the road. Which is the exact thing the mothers told us never to do or else we'll find out what OR ELSE really means. We're digging up the gold that's glinting in the sand so we'll be rich enough to buy the Froot Loops & Cocoa Krispies the mothers can't afford to pay the dentist bills for. But the gold flakes into bits like dandruff (we didn't know it was really mica). So we head across the road to mine the other side.

And out of nowheres there's a logging truck on top of us, horn blaring, engine thundering, brakes squealing.

Suddenly I'm thrown hard to the ground. Crushed. Dead maybe. Only when I open my eyes it ain't Jesus I see—it's you. You tackled me & Merle, flew us under your arms into the ditch. Blood all down your legs where you skinned across the tar. Truck rolling off in the distance like nothing ever happened. And "Nothing ever happened" is what you says too.

"Don't you ever tell Mama or Daddy about this, or you'll wish that truck did hit you."

Me & the Truck That Almost Hit Me

Merle & me never told no one and never mentioned it to each other again, till it turned into something I might think I dreamt. If your suntan didn't skip over them splotchy white scars on your legs. Mama still goes TSK every summer and says, "That was some fall you took offen that bike, Ash."

I never worked harder to make you proud of me than I did practicing for that spring concert. Cause music's the thing you love best. But then I didn't know you wasn't gonna BE at my concert. I won't get all MELO-DRAMATIC on you and drip tears on the page to make you feel guilty, even though I could if I spent any time remembering how lousy it felt to play in front of all them faces and none of them yours. Had me so shook up, I played with vibrato after all. But not the good kind.

I don't wanna think about this no more—it's giving me a headache. I'm gonna watch TV.

January 4

Libby's Motor Lodge & Campground is what they call a "family business." One reason is, it grew right out of the kitchen. At 1st the Daigles thought Daddy was adding on a 4th bedroom so you & me wouldn't have to share. Which there've been times I wished he was.

Daddy built the units room by room, hammering away all morning after working all night at the blueberry cannery. At 10 rooms, Daddy quit the blueberries to tend office and putter around the place full-time. It ain't a bad life. Course, Grammy Ethyl likes to wink at me and say Daddy owes his good fortune to Pudgy Lovell getting religion. He become so obsessed with saving Daddy's soul during coffee breaks that Daddy become obsessed with getting into a new line of work.

From the very beginning, Mama had me delivering breakfast baskets to the customers. "What a cunning kid," they'd say. If they was from Maine. If they was outa-staters they'd say, "How cute." Which I never thought nothing of till that fountain of English Miss Small told us we should know for our own good how certain vocabulary here in Maine ain't used in the rest of the nation. North of the Kittery Bridge kids are CUNNING, but on the New Hampshire side they're CUTE (and foxes are cunning). Here moose and some people are GAWMY, but everywhere else they're UNCOORDINATED. You STAVED IN the Blazer, but some wild driver from another state woulda WRECKED it.

I also do most of the housework cause Mama has to housekeep the units. Deena use to till she went on strike and negotiated a better deal. "I'd rather dig grubs than swab strangers' body scraps out of bathtubs," she says.

"Fine," says Daddy. "You can do all the digging you want—the grounds could use a good weeding. While you're at it, plant some flowers & trim the shrubs, keep the grass mowed, the leaves raked, the snow shoveled & the pool vacuumed."

Libby's Motor Lodge & Campground with Free
Pool & Satellite TV!

21

"Well, that ain't bad, for prison labor," Deena says. "At least I can work on my tan."

The campground was your idea. "Ash's baby," Daddy called it, so you had to take care of it. (The satellite dish was my baby, and I give it plenty of attention.)

You needed more than $30/week allowance to pay for college, so you started working at the blueberry factory the Monday after you graduated. But I didn't mind that you quit your family job and I had to do it and miss reran reruns of the Big 3—<u>The Beverly Hillbillies</u>, <u>The Brady Bunch</u>, and <u>Gilligan's Island.</u> MY allowance went up 300%. What I minded was, you quit the FAMILY. You was like Calvin Cove—blink and you'll miss it. No, I take that blink back, cause only a deaf person could miss it whenever you was home. You was locked in the bathroom getting ready to go out, blasting the Top 40 from my breadbox till the house shook.

"Mr. Ash, lower the babel a few decibels!" Mama says.

"Just a minute," you'd yell back.

Then, after a few minutes of no change, "Ashton Allen Libby, you're deafening <u>bo-coo</u> sets of perfectly good ears. Including customers'!" Mama has such a good Maine accent, a stranger'd never know she grown up so near the Quebec border that she learnt English as a 2nd language. But she does occasionally speak French to dress up the fact that she's perturbed.

"Just a minute," you'd yell. Again.

Deena enjoyed pounding the door and screaming at

you. Her favorites was, "Get that dumb-ASH outa there" and "I'm gonna kick some ASH." Then Mama'd scream at Deena—Mama's not the screaming type, but the bathroom acoustics wasn't on her side—"I told you a million times not to talk like that!"

Your baby-oily baths clogged up the drain & left an ungodly ring. We went through Liquid-Plumr like it was milk. My biceps grown an inch from scrubbing the tub. Course, you locking yourself in there had one advantage—I didn't get much chance to practice violin. Could've done it in kitchen acoustics, but Mama was born with a good ear and didn't want me developing mine in hers.

One night Daddy pounded on the bathroom door. "I gotta get in there now, Ash."

"Just a minute."

Pound. Pound. "I gotta get IN THERE."

"Just a minute."

POUND. POUND. POUND. "Stop that friggin' and fartin' around and let me in right THIS *#%@ MINUTE! Listen, I'm unbuckling my belt!"

A few just-a-minutes later Daddy run to the Blazer and peeled out to the campgrounds bathhouse to do his business.

"Dayna, Wesley, I'm putting you on notice right now," he says when he got back. "You ain't allowed to go through this stage of adolescence the same way as Ash. You think up some other way to be a growing pain."

"Sure Daddy," I says. "Glad you still have a sense of humor."

"Growing pains, my ASH," says Deena. "There's only I reason I can think of for him needing 3 baths a day, and that's Krista Belotte."

"That right?" says Daddy. "In that case maybe I oughta start taking 3 baths a day and blasting music."

"Daddy you're DISGUSTING," says Deena.

Krista's awful good-looking. Long blond hair, green eyes, the skinniest waist you ever seen on someone with curves. Smart! And nice on top of it.

You'd never forget Krista Belotte, would you, Ash? In the middle of the night after a graduation party, you told me she was your Ist & only true love, and then you made me swear never to tell a soul you admitted that, even Krista, which is another reason nobody else better ever read this composition book, and if anyone besides Ash has got this far, Merle Daigle, you better stop right now OR I'LL HAUNT YOU WITH CHAINS AND BRING HELP!

January 5

People who wanted to stay at Libby's over 4th of July use to book a room or a site years ahead of time cause we thrown the best party anywheres. Lobsters straight out of the traps from Gull Rock, peas & baby potatoes fresh from Grammy Ethyl's garden, warm pool, cold coolers, good view of the VFW fireworks, and the Upcountry

Boys jamming. The fun really started when Grammy Ethyl loosed her inhibitions and howled out "Stand By Your Man" while dancing the 2-step with a lobster. She'd keep saying, "I ain't had so much fun in 40-11 years." Which is Grammy for "in my whole life." Guess she didn't like the sound of 51, back when she was.

I'll never forget the 4th a few years back when you surprised the Upcountry Boys with the Knights of Sisyphus T-shirts you'd made, then tried to talk them into changing their name.

The Knights of Sisyphus T-Shirt

"Why would we wanna do a foolish thing like that?" says the Boys.

"Cause I read in a mythology book how there was this legendary king of Corinth named Sisyphus who was condemned to roll a rock up a hill in Hades," you says, "only to have it roll back down again every time he got near the top. Well, you know the Knights of Columbus, right? The Knights of Sisyphus are like them, only instead of being Catholics they wanna be country music stars. They know it's useless, but they keep at it anyways."

"Ain't Ash a smart little shit," says the Boys, but that was the only time they worn your T-shirt.

The year you hit the moose, the 4th of July was drizzly and chilly, but the party started off like all the rest anyways. Like a good dream that's been coming back again & again for so long that you take it for granted, never suspecting this might be the last time.

The picnic was digesting, the Boys was getting the instruments set up, and Grammy was starting to hum when you & Deena stood in front of the office with your backs to the crowd and made throat static so everyone would simmer down and watch you.

"Hold on to your hat—here comes THE ASH BREEZE," someone hollered.

"This is the 4th of July at Libby's Motor Lodge & Campground with Free Pool & Satellite TV!" you & Deena says. "And we's the Juggs." Then you turned to the crowd and started singing country-twang harmony like the Judds before the mother got hepatitis B, you playing guitar and Deena holding up a Narragansett empty for a mike. You was singing falsetto and dancing around to show off the 2 balloons stuffed up your shirt. Having fun with family & friends just like old times. My heart was hugging up to my ribs while I watched you acting out. Krista's face was all lit up sweet like cotton candy. Merle laughed—the Boys, The Hormone, the customers laughed. Everybody laughed except the fuddy-duddies from 7. Their frowns was stiff, glued on. Their heads bent together and they whispered while the rest of the crowd hooted.

Mama seen them too, and then she weren't laughing. She waved her arms to catch your eye. When you looked towards her, she rolled her eyes towards Mr. & Mrs. Fuddy-Duddy, as if to say, "PSST, Sir Ashton Libby, the customer's always right."

If Daddy weren't in a unit unclogging a toilet, maybe you'd of stopped. He coulda give you his stone-faced stare that use to make his wish your command. But Daddy weren't there for the Mt. Rushmore look, so you winked at Mama and kept on singing. Then you danced yourself over to the couple from 7 and plunked right down in Mr. Fuddy's lap.

And kissed his nose. Now it just seems crass, but at the moment it was hilarious. People was slapping their knees & roaring. Except Mrs. Duddy, of course. And Mama. Her eyes was slots.

You looked square at Mama but didn't flinch. You got up, shook your balloons in the man's face, and finished the song on a high note. While you & Deena was bowing and the audience was giggling & wolf-whistling, the Fuddy-Duddies huffed off to 7.

5 minutes later Daddy bolted out of the office and hauled you off by your belt loops.

The couple from 7 wasn't long for Libby's Motor Lodge & Campground. Next time I seen Daddy, he had a faceful of them little red spiders that pop out when his temper bursts. The next few days I lost count of the times he nagged you through the bathroom door about paying him back the $120 he lost on 4th of July weekend.

"Just a minute," you says.

January 6

I don't think you remember much of the stuff that was going on around in here. Which is one reason I'm writing it down. If you do remember any, I hope reading it don't bore you.

Me & Deena go to the Cavalry Bible Church every Sunday cause Mama makes us. Use to make you too, till—no, I'm ahead of myself.

Mama goes to church cause she loves the place. Lifts her spirits week to week, she says. And she can sing loud without nobody complaining. That's one reason we don't go to the Catholic church over to Machias like Grammy & Grampy Tibbetts want. That church don't sing much. Also, Catholic's 30 miles—Cavalry's 300 yards. Besides, it ain't every church next door that's got an old buddy in the pulpit, even if the friendship's all moldy.

Grammy Ethyl always winks and says Pudgy Lovell wanted Daddy with him in heaven so bad that he built his church where Daddy'd hear the bells call him every Sunday, "Save-Steve! Save-Steve! Save-Steve!"

"Jesus H. Christ, Bonnie, I'm all for a little religion, but I don't know how you can set there listening to that crackpot every week," says Daddy. "The way I understand it, God give us FREE CHOICE to live by. But to Pudgy Lovell, the only choice is his way or hell. Which ain't much of a selection."

"Ain't Daddy a fart smella," Deena whispered to me.

"Well now," says Mama, "you use to call his personality CHARISMA. You're gonna get opinionated ideas in every church. At least at Cavalry I can figure out where the Bible ends and Bradley begins."

Every week Pastor leaps all around in God's word— on your Mark, get set, Matthew Isaiah Numbers Etc.— and Mama keeps up with him nose to nose. Flips pages, takes notes, nods like it all makes sense.

Makes me nod OFF. Unless it's a Don't-Roast-in-Hell Day.

Every few weeks, his eyes all to blazing, Pastor asks which direction you're taking to the hereafter—high road or low road? He describes how the low road will disgust all 5 of your senses, it's so ugly, stinking, bitter, noisy and HOT. "If your seat feels a little warm right about now," he says at the end, "that's God's little hint of what's to come in Satan's fiery furnace, God's way of letting you know you're a sinner just like the rest of us and need the loving grace of the Lord's forgiveness to spend eternity with him. Come on down to the front and get right with the Lord Jesus Christ." Them days folks get moving before Mrs. Pike can wind up her elbow.

Most of the time me & Merle pretend we're taking notes like Mama, but really we're writing new Bible verses. Merle's favorite is the 151st Psalm:

Now I lay me down to sleep
And pray the Lord I don't count sheep.
If I should lay there wide awake,
I pray the Lord some ZZZZZZs to make.

I don't need to tell you, do I Ash old boy, how much trouble I'd be in up to Cavalry if anyone else found out about this? Especially Mrs. Fish-Lips. The woman has commandments to stop sinning OPPORTUNITIES. "May I remind you, Mrs. Libby, of the Pike Commandment?" Every week after How's-that-Steve-Libby. "To prevent necking & petting and thereby avoid the road to adultery, Kenneth shalt not get closer than 10 feet to Deena without an adult chaperone."

Once Deena come back with, "In case you didn't know, Mrs. Pike, you can't commit ADULTERY if you ain't MARRIED."

The next week Mrs. Pike revised the Commandment, "To prevent getting closer than 10 feet without a chaperone, and thereby avoid the road to adultery, which includes any necking & petting outside of holy matrimony, Kenneth and Deena shalt not go on car dates by themself."

My favorite Bible verse, I writ along the edges of the apple part of Genesis. Never liked that chapter.

The Lord is my shepherd; I shall not want.
He maketh me to lie down in green pastures:
He leadeth me beside the still waters.
He restoreth my soul . . .

Bet you thought I was gonna make one up, huh? When everything's mixed up and turned around, ordinary things come as a surprise. I learnt that from what happened to you.

January 7

Funny, how that summer the weather was weird right along with you. No dog days of July & August. Just more April showers and extra blankets. At 1st business was still okay in the units, but there weren't exactly a stampede to stake tents out back. Which didn't bother me till the folks figured out they was losing $ on me and changed the groundskeeping wage to piecework, $1 per site. The best part was, the grass grown so fast Deena had her work CUT OUT for her. "Deena, the dandelions are growing like WEEDS from HADES," I says everyday at breakfast, "you better GO TO 'em."

Deena in the Weeds from Hades

"Wes, don't PLAGUE your sister," says Mama.
In other states, mothers say "Don't TEASE."
Right about now, Daddy would tell me to stop friggin' and fartin' around and get to the real point.
One morning in July, Deena was watching me & Mama fix the breakfast baskets—hot blueberry muffins, croissants, and a pot of coffee for each room—when you come home from the night before. Your hair poked off to the side like it was starched. Except the ends was sag-

ging from the drizzle you run through. Your shirt was buttoned 2 holes off. You smelt of cigarettes, beer, and puke. Mostly puke.

DEENA: "Well, look what the cat drug in."
MAMA: "Ash!"
ASH: "Mama!"
MAMA: "Wes! Deena! You 2 go deliver the baskets now."
DEENA: "Aw Mama, that ain't MY—"
MAMA: "Now!"

So I didn't get to hear Mama bawl you out. But I known she was gonna, cause the look on her face didn't say, "Good morning Ash, how nice to see you Ash."

When I was outside 6, I seen Mama's umbrella storming up the road. She always walks off her mad spells. I was knocking on 7 when you started sharing your music with the world. Good thing for you that Daddy was making a delivery to the town dump, or you woulda been dog food.

The pudgy gray woman who opened the door was still in her robe. "Where's that racket coming from?" Her nose scrunched.

I shrugged.

"$40 a night oughta buy a person some peace and quiet," comes a yell from the john.

I didn't say nothing, just held out the basket to the woman. She took it and smiled halfway. "We had teenagers once. I understand these things, but maybe you better see about that noise before Fritz gets too worked up."

Inside, the house rocked with the beat. It made me ugly, you being such a jerk. Ruining my idea of you. A guy like you shouldn't let people down, Ash—that's what I was thinking, and I was gonna tell you too. Had my fist raised to pound on the bathroom door when the music stopped.

This is one of them things I'm positive you don't remember.

"Shut up! Shut your damn trap!" Your voice sounded panicky. And I hadn't even said nothing yet.

"I said SHUT UP!"

Then come a crash. Then glass shattering. Then you was breathing scared behind the door.

It scared ME to think someone was in there with my brother, maybe hurting you! I beat on the door.

"Ash! Ash! There someone else with you? You okay?"

No "just a minute" this time—you opened the door. You looked petrified. Bloodless. Wet hair, towel around your waist.

"Ash?! What happened!"

"Didn't you hear it?" Words dragging along.

"I heard heavy metal blasting my ears and then that window over there breaking," I says, heading over to look through the broken pane. My breadbox was on the ground having a rain shower.

"You didn't hear?" you says, even slower than before. "Judas the Betrayer was talking to me on the radio."

I checked out your face to see if this was one of your jokes. But you looked all washed out, not a hint of smart aleck in them eyes. I felt limp, seeing you like that and realizing that you actually meant it. Judas the Betrayer ain't no rock group.

Shawn Fox, a guy in my grade who smokes pot for breakfast, use to say crazy stuff like that till he got sent off to reform school. I figured you'd been conducting some chemical experiments that wasn't good for your brain. "Ash my man, you need some sleep," I says.

After I got you into bed, I called you in sick to the blueberry factory so you wouldn't lose your job. Then I went and brought my breadbox in. All wet & scratched up, but it still worked.

Deena wanted to know what the crashing noise was, Mama wanted to know why the house was hosting a mosquito convention, and Daddy wanted to know what cost him a pane of glass, a tube of putty & an hour of extra work. But I didn't say nothing except, "Ask Ash."

You slept till Mama sent me to wake you up for lunch. You looked 1000% better.

"Breaking the window was an accident," you says. "I was practicing my Mick Jagger impression in front of the mirror. Sorry Mum, Dad."

Not a word about Judas the radio announcer. But I didn't say nothing. That was yours to tell.

January 8

For years you played guitar with the Upcountry Boys Friday & Saturday nights. Remember how we all tagged along back when you started? The folks'd get Grammy Ethyl to tend Libby's so we wouldn't miss a minute of you playing. At any wedding receptions we weren't invited to, Mama & Daddy listened from the car parked close to a window. They also listened to me & Deena in the backseat begging to go in or go home, which is why it didn't take them long to give up on wedding receptions. After a few years they even give up on dance halls, unless they was in a party mood. And then they'd drag me or Deena along "cause he's your brother."

That Saturday you broke the window, Mama decided she had some dancing to get out of her system. She got up from the dinner table and flapped herself around to the Hank Williams Jr. song on the radio. Mama has this affair of the feet going on with Hank Williams Jr. Which started when he debuted on The Ed Sullivan Show at age 14. Mama says she was just 5 or 6 then, but I can add & subtract.

"Steve, let's go up to the VFW and boogie," she says.

I'm thinking it would be smarter to stay home and dance to the real Hank Williams Jr. CD in the living room than it would be to listen to the Upcountry Boys butcher

Hank Williams Jr. at the VFW hall. But "Them's party words," says Daddy. He grinned and run to the bathroom for a shower.

For once you wasn't in there. Already gone to set up the band.

"Why don't you go change into that cute jean skirt Grammy Ethyl made you for Christmas," Mama says to Deena. I sighed and leaned back. Major relief—her turn to go along.

"Darn, wouldn't you know it's stained?" says Deena. She hated that skirt. She told me it looked like a denim bed ruffle, and that made HER the bed.

MAMA: "Oh? I didn't notice you wearing it lately."
DEENA: "Someone spilt some red wine on it last time I wore it up to the VF. Forgot to put it in the wash."
MAMA: "That was back before the boys hit the moose! The stain'll never come out. Well, you can wear—"
DEENA: "Mama, I'd LOVE to spend the evening with you and Daddy, really I would, but I'm expecting company tonight."

It was something, I thought, how Deena could say that B.S. so casual you could actually believe it. But it didn't slip by Mama. Nothing much ever does. Except what was happening to you.

MAMA: "Miss Dayna Libby! No parents home, no Hormone in the house."

DEENA: "Ma-am-maa! The name's DEENA, and I hate it when you call Kenneth THAT!"
MAMA: "If the shoe fits."

I seen where Deena wanted this bickerment to lead—me straight up to the VF while she stayed home with you-know-who. Now don't get me wrong, Ash. I love your guitar playing, but my baby satellite dish was just crying out for attention. So I says, "Deena, how about you invite The KENNETH to boogie with you at the VFW? Mrs. Pike should appreciate all them VETERAN chaperones."

If Deena's eyes was arrows I'd of been in a pool of blood on the floor.

"Now, that's an idea." Mama ruffled my hair. "Give Kenny a call," she says to Deena, "if you want to see him tonight."

Deena stuck her tongue out at me on her way to the phone.

I got me a bowl of popcorn, a liter of soda, a bag of candy, the remote, & stretched out on the couch for a night of TV. None of Mama's REPEATS such as: "The living room couch is for sitting. If you want to eat, go to the kitchen. If you want to lie down, go to bed." Nobody to yell at me for hopping channels. No vacancies at Libby's. Paradise.

Between MTV & baseball scores & stand-up comics I watched the original black & white <u>Franken-stein.</u> Nothing like the cartoons. Did you know Franky was really the doctor, not the monster? Near the end of the movie I fell asleep, but I was dreaming <u>Frankenstein</u> in black & white and didn't know I was sleeping until the door slammed and you stormed by. Your guitar case banged the lamp table and woke me up good, in a bad mood. I says, "Ash! What's up, jerk?"

You just kept going and slammed yourself into our room. I shut off the TV to follow you, and silence dropped over my head like a winter hat. I realized the rain had stopped. A car pulled up quiet, and the doors shut even more quiet, Mama style, saving the perfectly good dreams of our customers. I went to open the door—the folks usually do alot of fumbling for keys at the end of their boogie evenings. Mama & Daddy rushed in, didn't even say, "Hi honey, we're home."

MAMA: "Did Ash come in?"
WES: "Just now and in a real lousy mood."
MAMA: "Thank God he's home."
DADDY: "I don't know what's got into that kid."
WES: "What'd Ash do?"
MAMA: "Well . . ." (Stalling.) "I guess you could say he . . ."
DEENA: "S-ripped off his Knights of Syphilis shirt and walked off the—HIC—stage in the middle of—HIC—'Take This Job &—HIC HIC—Shove It.'"

It didn't take a genius to figure out Deena'd dipped her ladle in the wrong punch bowl. No wonder she'd been holding the wall up and her lips closed. Ordinarily a situation like that would trigger Daddy's drill sergeant routine and Mama's French. But right then they hardly seemed to care.

And that was the night you quit the band.

January 9

We're into stuff you definitely don't remember too good. Nothing too good about most of this stuff anyways.

"What you mean, you ain't going to church," says Mama the next day at 10:24 A.M. She was in her yellow flower dress, standing over Deena's bed. Deena was a giant lump under a hot pink comforter. (Don't tell her I said GIANT.) I was all dressed up, hair slicked back with water even though it'd be back across my forehead soon's it dried.

"I ain't going to church. That's what I mean!" Deena's yell got swallowed by the pillow over her head. Sounded far away.

The church bell clanged the 5 minute warning. Sharp sound against the dull noise of rain. "Save-Steve! Save-Steve! Save-Steve!"

"I think she means she ain't going to church," I says from the doorway. It was hard to resist.

"Thank you very much Wesley William Libby HOLMES," Mama says. Squinting sarcasm across the room.

"Mum, you know exactly what Deena means." You was behind me, adjusting your neck vise, AKA necktie.

Nobody'd know by looking at you what you done the night before.

"She doesn't want to sit in a pew with the rest of the hypocrites and get hellfired and damnationed all morning by the pastor impostor. Can't you see that Bradley Lovell is really a game show host? 'Come on down—you're the next repentant on the new <u>Christ Is Right</u>'!"

On HYPOCRITES you give me a spit shower and stared meaningful at Mama. Her jaw dropped so low, I seen the fillings winking. I woulda laughed at the game-show-host part, but Mama's eyes looked too pitiful. Surprised. Hurt. Mama, a hypocrite, Ash? What was wrong with you?

The brother I use to know wouldn't of said that stuff, and if he did he woulda took it back for Mama's sake. The brother I use to know volunteered to take me & Merle to the fair so the folks wouldn't have to stand around pretending their smiles was real while we bobbed up & down on fake horsies. The brother I use to know gave Mama & Daddy gifts like "Romantic Weekend for 2 in Rm. 10 of Libby's Motor Lodge, all expenses paid, to include but not limited to child care, tending office, housekeeping & making breakfast baskets."

You smiled devilish. You stripped off your tie. You stretched like a sleepy dog and you says, "Some of the most faithful never pass through a church door. Fanatics are fools. I'm going back to bed." The door slammed.

Somehow I weren't surprised when Mama did NOT say, "What you mean, you're going back to bed." She just stood there a moment with her eyes shut. I think she was praying.

Deena's hand fumbled around outside the covers till it pinched Mama's skirt. Her head poked out from the comforter, and her arm pulled Mama's legs into a tight hug. Like a toddler afraid of a stranger.

"Don't listen to him, Mama," she says. Voice stuffed up, pathetic. "I ain't going to church cause I'm too hung-over to stand up."

January 15

You probably noticed I been ripping out pages right & left. Don't worry, Ash—it ain't secret stuff I don't want you to know. It's stuff I wanna forget. You try writing down stuff you wanna forget and see how many pages you rip up. It ain't just that the words are hard to get right. Words on paper seem more real than words shoved back behind your ears somewheres. Writ words bring it all back. And IT made me want to hate you.

If this was an English assignment, Miss Small would write, "What's IT?" Well, IT's the stuff I keep ripping out. Things that happened. Things I felt.

Don't you think they got Maine all wrong on TV? Like <u>Murder, She Wrote.</u> It ain't just the accents they frig up, it's the TRAILERS. Getting stuck behind Molasses drivers 1/3 of the time, anyone can see there's certain

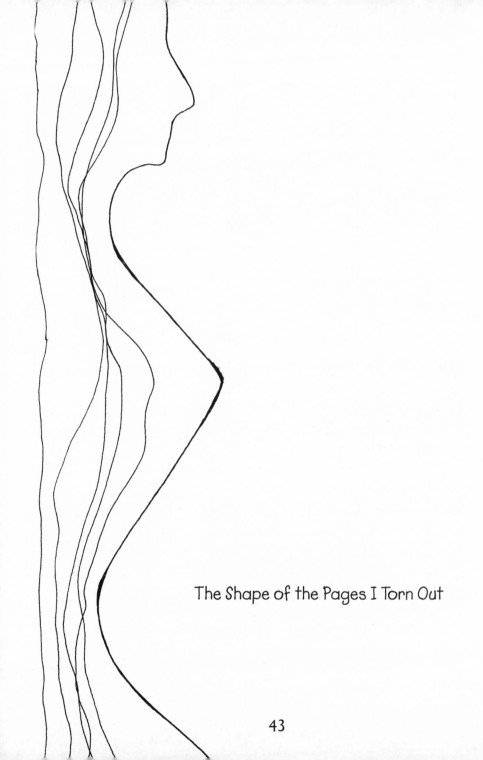

The Shape of the Pages I Torn Out

44

laws of trailers around here. Such as, if you pass a big beautiful house like Jessica Fletcher's, the next place will ALWAYS be a trailer. The only thing Maine's got more of than trailers is PICKUPS. Sometimes the pickup is bigger than the trailer.

There's your trailer that's trying to hide behind overgrown shrubs. Then there's your run-down, overrun-with-junk trailer with tar glopped down the sides from roof patching—this trailer don't got the sense to hide. But your typical Maine trailer is trying to be a house. Like Grammy Ethyl's. She put a cellar under it, a pitched roof over it, an addition onto it, and a deck out back of it. Grammy's got that trailer fixed up REAL NICE.

Grammy's Trailer

The Daigles also got a trailer trying to be a house, only theirs is trying to be an ESTATE. It's also trying to be CHRISTIAN.

I seen trailers attached to a real house, with a

The Daigle Estate

greenhouse, attached to each other's back doors, made into a 3-family apartment building and remodeled into a log home.

Log Home (Trailer Incognito)

The RED BARN REDEMPTION CENTER (where bottles & cans get SAVED) is actually a trailer—the barn where the owners live is out back. Guess the TRAILER

REDEMPTION CENTER ain't got the right ring. People over there don't ask me about you no more. Mostly they look away.

God, there was days I wished I could hate you, ASH. Like pretty near the whole year I was 14. Like now. Hating you would make this writing easy. Whenever I get hate-teeked off at someone, I tell them off in a letter. The next day I rip it up, and the hate's gone, ripped up. That makes the teeked off part easier to square away. I thought writing you this book would be that way, but it ain't. There's lots of ripping up, but there ain't much easy. And nothing squared away.

January 16

Love writes even easier than hate. Last summer there was this girl in 9 for a whole week—she had a HOT PINK bikini and RED hair. I couldn't stop thinking about her, but I couldn't let on I was crazy in love with her, neither. I mean I literally COULDN'T. Everyday when I says, "Hi," it come out like I was saying "Aaah" under a tongue depressor. I didn't dare try for a complete sentence, but I writ all my feelings down in a hot pink letter. The next day I ripped it up, and you know what? The crazy was gone, ripped up. That left the love part easy to square away. Without the crazy part, love is spelled I-N-F-A-T-U-A-T-I-O-N. (I was infatuated with 9's color scheme.)

Remember when Krista used all her Scrabble letters

to make FAT into INFATUATED? She won that game even though she lost a turn for playing UGSOME, which ain't a word no more but use to mean repulsive.

Love. I loved Togo the minute I seen him. The summer I turned 5. It weren't crazy or infatuation, neither. Us kids begged & begged for a dog till Daddy & Mama broke down and brung home this flop-eared pup the neighbors was gonna drown cause they didn't know who the father was. CUNNING! But you could tell by his ears his father weren't no pedigree, even though the rest of him looked pure German shepherd like his mother. The only papers he had was newspapers.

Too bad Togo acted like the ears part of him. Not obedient. Never got out of the habit of chewing things. Shoes, rugs, chair legs, woodwork. Remember how he chewed the folks' mattress and dragged the stuffing around the house? Mama spoke some French I never heard before and took a very long walk. Daddy held Togo's nose in the stuffing and cuffed his tail end.

Us kids built a doghouse—Deena made curtains—out back where there was nothing to chew except trees. (We shoulda got him a little trailer instead—it woulda fit right in.) We tied Togo up with strong rope. Not strong enough. He gnawed himself loose, chased a deer through Millard Worcester's blueberries, then stopped to chew on Millard's cat. While Daddy was at the vet's paying the bill, he had Togo put to sleep to get him out of the chewing habit for good. Brung him home in a closed carton.

"When we gonna wake him up?" I says.

Daddy laughed. Which made me cry cause suddenly I got why it was funny. Then Daddy got why I was crying, and he almost cried for laughing at me.

You was all riled up when you got home from school and found out what was in the box.

"You killed a dog for acting like a dog?" you says. "Would you put me to sleep if you didn't like how I acted?"

"No, but I'd put you to BED."

"Daddy!"

"I'm sorry, Ash—you're right," says Daddy. "This ain't the time for kidding. You gotta understand, once a dog's got a craving to chase deer & maul cats, nothing can get it out of his blood. But you're my boy, and I know YOU got good blood." Daddy tried to hug you, but you pulled away.

"You coulda put Togo on a CHAIN," you says.

Daddy nodded, and his cheeks puffed in & out as he waited for the right answer. Finally he says, "Would you like to live at the end of a chain? Even if you was a dog?"

You didn't say nothing, just got tear sparkles in your eyes and shook your head. I didn't know why at the time—personally I'd of gone for the chain instead of the box. Still would. But now I see the sad of it. Chained ain't no way to live.

We buried Togo next to the doghouse. My lst funeral. Grammy Ethyl's mama (Great-Grammy Avis) died around then too, but they wouldn't let me go to that one. I never met her. No kids allowed in her apartment, which I found out last year was in the Bangor Mental Health Institute. I'll explain that another day.

Grampy Libby was my 2nd funeral. I was 10. Remember how he use to tease darling Deena so perfect she couldn't think of nothing to say back? He was so good at everything. Folks always said you took after him—he taught you guitar & cribbage. My word I loved him, and look, I've lived without him 5 years now. You know what that means, Ash? I could, if I had to—I hate to say it but it must be true if I done it with Togo and I done it with Grampy—I COULD live without you.

January 17

PARADOX: contradictory yet true. I looked it up when Krista got the X on a triple-letter-score playing Scrabble. A secret is one. You get a kick out of knowing something nobody else knows and putting it over on people who think they know more than you, but at the same time you wish you could tell so they'd find out how they got put over. Paradox.

Right this minute I'm writing on the paradox floor.

See, Merle & me got this secret place we built a mile and 2/10ths back in the woods behind the campsites, in the government preserve. Well, we didn't exactly build it.

What we did was remodel. When we was little squirts we always played Justice League of America and flew off to discover disasters to rescue people from. One day we traipsed so far we'd of been in deep manure if a grown-up Daigle or Libby found out, and we discovered a disaster to rescue. An ancient one-room log cabin.

The windows and door was long gone, and the floor was laid straight on the ground. When we stepped inside, our feet mushed through the rot like the boards was moss. Stink! Like a moldy litter box for moose. In the corner there was a cot that actually moved with all the mice living in the mattress. Cobwebs all over. Squirrel's nest in the fireplace. And a trunk full of old stuff including the '60s comic books Merle & me told everyone we found real cheap at a gar(b)age sale.

The roof was good, maybe cause the shingles was slate and the beams was 12-inch logs. The walls was good too, except the bottom row of logs sogged into the dirt.

Everyday after that we spent hours reaming the place out. We evicted the mice and squirrel with some of Merle's mother's D-Con. The place smelt better after we dug up the floor and Cloroxed all the walls. We covered the window holes with the thick plastic insulation Merle's father dug offen the side of their trailer in the spring. And we used the cardboard box from Grammy's new refrigerator to make a door. Then we built us a new floor.

You know the scrap lumber of Daddy's that kept disappearing when he was building the bathhouse? Well, we never took nothing he coulda used. Scrap by scrap Merle & me hauled the lumber a mile and 2/10ths.

We known from listening to Daddy building, "A good carpenter's gotta keep wood off the ground and on the level. Plumb. Square."

"Plumb, dumb," says Merle.

"Square, I don't care," I says. That's how little we was. Dr. Seuss was king.

We covered the ground with slate from the tumbledown wall at the edge of Millard Worcester's field. Then we framed in our floor with warped 2 x 4's, fit together the odd plywood scraps like puzzle pieces, and nailed them down. Our floor weren't plumb, but it was sturdy, and it didn't stink.

That cabin is the world's biggest secret, Ash, which I've kept for 7 years. We called it the Secret Place till Pastor Pudgy had this word SHIBBOLETH laid on him in a sermon, meaning "a test word for the enemy." Me & Merle just looked at each other and grinned.

I'm telling you about the Shibboleth cause I'd hate to see my 1/2 of it go to waste after I die. Merle already has 1/2—why leave it all to him? Somebody in the family oughta be able to go there and enjoy it like I have.

From our house the ocean is heavy to smell, faint to hear if the wind's right, but impossible to see. Stand on the tippy-top of the Shibboleth roof and you can see the ocean for miles. It's the best thing I got to pass on in the world. And it's a secret. See what I mean about paradox?

Listen, Ash. I gotta tell you the stuff I gotta tell you, even if you don't wanna believe it, but you can always turn the page or shut the book or burn the damn thing if you don't wanna know the truth. We didn't get no pages to turn or shut or burn—we had to live it. We didn't know where things was heading or how they'd turn out, so you got an advantage.

Here goes. What happened that day in church. I'll just come out and say it, and I ain't ripping this page out.

They was real happy at Cavalry when Bonnie Libby sneaked in late—no Deena, no Ash. Pastor was already past the Program Announcements and onto Welcome Strangers. The heads tipped towards us in a wave, then they tipped back together in 2s, like animals whispering on Noah's Ark. I was too embarrassed to go squeeze in with Merle. I hid behind Mama.

Mrs. Pike give us the fishy look when Mama & me slid into her pew. The Hormone was a wet lump of misery on the other side of her. If Deena was too hungover to stand up, don't ask me how he got his tail all the way up to church. Swayed through (not TO) the hymns.

There's lots of Sundays that Pastor points to his pile of yellow paper and says, "If I delivered this entire message, it would take 2 hours and the roast you left in the oven would dry up before you got home. So on the way to church I prayed the Lord would provide me with something short & sweet. Brethren, I'm here to tell you the Lord answers prayers, cause he just laid a message on me that'll take only 20 minutes." Everyone always laughs, but kind of a nervous laugh, cause when the Lord lays a message on Pastor, it always feels like the devil. The man's eyes got X-ray vision for sin. That day he aimed them straight at MAMA and says, "The Lord appreciates a perfect roast." My stomach wanted to get up and leave.

I can't tell you the whole message cause after the 1st few sentences my head burnt out. What the Lord laid on Pastor was, Satan snuck into the VFW hall Saturday night and stretched his evil tentacles aholt of some young people who shouldn't of been there. The body's a temple and you don't see Jesus taking no 6-pack into the temple or dancing cheek-to-cheek with Mary Magdalen to "All My Ex's Live in Texas."

Mama set still as a chair and stared down at a page of Psalms.

Pastor ended up saying the individuals involved can still send the devil shrieking back to the pit by coming down to the front this Sunday if they're here—his eyes making a laser beam to The Hormone—and next Sunday if they ain't—he looked at me cause I was looking at him—and inviting Jesus back into their hearts, and nobody except him would ever know they come on down cause the congregation would bow their heads in prayer and he'd never mention no names.

I bowed my head and prayed this would all be over (the most humiliating 20 minutes of my life) (up till then). But it didn't help Kenneth stay anonymous since Mrs. Pike drug him over my knees to get him up front. Out of the bottom of my eyes, I watched him limp along, and I seen something else too. Most of him and Deena's youth group was limping right after him! Including Merle's sister Belinda. I put 2 + 2 together and got a going-on-senior party drinking their heads off.

While Mama & me jostled along with the crowd on the way out, we heard talk that put Ash Libby & family to blame for the whole thing. Such as:

"I always thought them Libbys was asking for trouble letting Ash run around with that band."

"And letting their other kids run around after him."

"Seems everyone's kids was running around after him. Praise the good Lord he quit!"

"I always wondered about that boy and his Knights of Sisyphus ideas. Them's the devil's work, alrite!"

"Is it true what I heard, how filthy his mouth was last night?"

"Shocking! I know cause I heard all about it from someone who was there."

Mama whispered to me between her teeth, "SHE was there. Half the town was there, and IRATE that Ash quit."

It didn't make me feel no better that you had a point about hypocrites.

January 19

This is the absolute last time I tell you, DAIGLE, eyes off this book or ELSE. There are unthinkable ways of haunting that I'll find out after I die. If you read this God's gonna getcha, mark my words. THIS TIME I AIN'T KIDDING!!!!!!!

This Means
You, Merle!

January 20

That same Sunday night I was half-asleep, the house settling into late black quiet, when you flamed up a match and lit a cigarette. You'd been smoking like an incinerator lately, made our room smell worse than trash. I wished my numb mouth was as smart as Deena's so I'd dare say, "In case you didn't know, this air belongs to my lungs too, and my lungs don't like breathing in CANCER." Daddy started smoking his cigarettes outdoor after she said that to him.

You took a deep drag and whooshed out the smoke slow and loud.

"I hate Mum," you says.

"Huh?" Thought I weren't hearing right.

"I hate mind readers," you says. "And I know Mum's been reading minds. I tested her."

I snorted a laugh. That Ash, I was thinking—he can be so dry sometimes, nobody can tell he's joking till his lips curl and give it away. But I couldn't see in the dark that there weren't no curl.

"She sure known what you was thinking about the woman in 10 you was OGLING," I says with a snicker. You hadn't gone out all day—for once—just set by the pool with the family and tourists. Behind Mama & Daddy's back Deena was running a betting pool, 50¢ each and the pot going to whoever come closest to guessing what time the clouds would start leaking on us again.

You spent the afternoon staring at 10—she was trying to fry herself in the lukewarm sun and didn't seem to notice that her bathing suit woulda made a better shoelace. You was ignoring everyone else like they didn't exist, but Mama talked at you anyways. Told you to get your eyes back in your head before they got dried out, ogling out in the warm air like that, the day after you got the whole town to running down the Libby name, a SUNDAY.

Your sheets rustled—you was turning over to grind

your cigarette out on the TV tray between the beds. "I was not ogling that woman," you says. "Not like you think. Mum said that to throw me off, so I wouldn't know she was mind reading."

I grunted so you'd explain.

"She's smart, but not smart enough to trick me," you says. "She shouldn't have said anything about Sunday. See, it told me she knew what I was really thinking."

You paused. I grunted again.

"I wasn't staring at that WOMAN, Wesley," you snapped. "I was just STARING, thinking about God. The real God, not Mr. Lovell's and Mrs. Pike's. God, Sunday, get it?"

"Oh," I says. "Yeah. I guess."

"Can you keep a secret, Wes?"

GRUNT.

"God has made the ways of truth known to me. I can't tell you any details yet, but when the time is right. . . ."

All my life that room had always felt safe. The safest place in the world, our room. But that night—

Let me put it this way, Ash old boy. A clan of bogeymen might as well have moved right in.

Mama weren't no mind reader, Ash. If she was, she'd of known to be scared of your thoughts.

I didn't believe you was going through a stage. Not no more. I lain awake thinking about your crazy ways—don't get mad at that word <u>crazy</u>—till your breathing got deep and heavy.

The next night Grammy Ethyl come ramming in right after her ritual Monday hair appointment, her curls all cemented into place for the week, and says, "Why didn't nobody tell me Ash quit the Upcountry Boys? You could've called—don't I call you whenever there's news and even when there isn't? I never been so embarrassed in my life as this morning when Lorene Lynch went on and on, 'I don't know how you do it, Ethyl,' she says, 'you raised them kids right—you'd think they'd know how to raise theirs, but . . .' Can you imagine! I just let her talk and didn't say anything to let on I didn't know my own family was stars of the latest gossip. If I'd known the facts, I'm sure I could've set the story straight and put an end to that Lorene Lynch's tiresome . . ."

Meanwhile, you was setting there acting like you never called Pastor Pudgy a game show host or Mama a mind reader. You just acted your usual weird. Washed a couple bagels down your throat with a pot of coffee, and lit up.

Grammy Ethyl was still narrating when Deena coughed out, "Hey, there, diaper rASH, you can trASH your own lungs if you want, but you ain't got no right to murder my grape clusters."

"Then Lorene had the nerve to say—GRAPE CLUSTERS?" says Grammy.

"Whatever! Them little breathing balloons in your

lungs," Deena snapped. She was in an ugly mood. Mama & Daddy just about give her the death sentence for getting drunk at the VFW. She couldn't go nowheres after dark for the rest of the summer, she couldn't have no pool parties, and no Hormone within 10 feet of her unless Mama &/or Daddy was IN BETWEEN.

I was all set to laugh at whatever smart remark you'd make back to Deena's balloons, but what you done was lean into her face and speak in smoke balls, "Alveoli." Then you grinned like a bad guy in a movie.

Mama almost choked on her coffee. "I'm shocked," she says. "This is not my son at the kitchen table. This is not the Ashton Allen Libby I raised. And while we're at it, HE wasn't at the VFW hall the other night, neither."

You was suddenly looking like Mr. Innocent. Out you come with, "Who, me?"

"I didn't raise you to act like a donkey, meuh-SYUH" (meaning you, Mr. Innocent-Face), "and you know what I'm talking about."

"It's a free world," you says with a big smile, "and YOU know what I'M talking about."

I didn't have to be a mind reader to know what YOU was talking about.

"FERM-may ta GUE-lay!" commanded Major Mama, pointing at you. She was WICKED pissed. She'd never say SHUT YOUR TRAP! in English, but she hollered it in Pig Latin French? Personally, I'd rather hear it in straight English so I don't have to wrestle a laugh down into my guts, but Mama can't admit that she's too stark raving mad to turn the other cheek. She shouldn't feel guilty about popping off—a person's only got 2 cheeks, and how long can you keep turning your neck like that?

You grinned the same way Merle does when he imitates Miss Small's arm flab waggling as she diagrams sentences on the board. Then you ground out your cigarette in your bagel plate and nodded outa the kitchen.

"Well, pardon me for living, you ASH-wipe," says Deena.

Grammy Ethyl cleared her throat and says, "Your father use to get his mouth washed out with soap flakes for that kind of language."

Mama rolled her eyes and took a deep breath. "Deena, I've told you a million times not to talk like that." Then, to Grammy, "Teenagers!"

"I didn't do nothing," I says.

"You'll be 14 in a few weeks," says Mama.

She made it sound like the flu.

January 22

"Insolent," announced Krista. "That's a triple-word score, and I used all my letters, so give me 74 points, Wes my friend."

I'm the only one in the family anyone trusts to keep score, and it ain't cause I'm the reincarnation of Al Einstein. I'm so honest, nobody knows when I ain't.

"Look that sucker up, Wes. Inso-whatever ain't a word—nobody can get 74 points out of 1-point letters," says Deena.

"Don't bother, brother, it's a word alrite," you says. "I'll use it in a sentence: Deena is insolent."

"Am not," says Deena. "Look it up, Wes."

I run my finger down the <u>insole-</u> words in <u>Webster's.</u> "I-N-S-O-L-E-N-T. Insultingly contemptuous in speech or conduct. Overbearing. Exhibiting boldness or—"

"That's enough stuttering, thank you," says Deena, slapping the book shut on my hand. "Your move, cow pASHture," she spit out at you.

Your Move, Cow

Your move, cow. Been a long time since I heard anyone say that. The story goes that I was in a car seat & there was a herd of Molasses cows in the middle of the road when I spoke my 1st sentence (Miss Small would call it my 1st sentence FRAGMENT). "Your move, cow." Cause I was always hearing "Your move, Bonnie/ Steve/Ash/Deena." After that the Scrabble slowpoke was always a COW.

Libbys & games use to go together like English teachers & poems. But not that summer cause of you being off somewheres every night, even though Mama & Daddy & me was always after you to stay home and do something with us, or at least stop driving yourself into the ground working all day and playing all night.

"Tomorrow," you'd say on your way out the door.

Tomorrow, my foot. After July 4th and the ogling Sunday, that night in August was the only evening you spent at home all summer. We wouldn't of been playing Scrabble that night, neither, except Krista made you.

I heard you 2 fighting in the driveway before you come in. Krista was ugly that you quit the Upcountry Boys in such a gross way that <u>Libby</u> was becoming a dirty word in Calvin Cove, as in, "Watch your Libby mouth." She was even more ugly that you was spending so much time at parties without her. Not that she wanted to go—surprise.

If Krista wasn't with you, that blew Deena's theory about why you needed 3 baths a day.

January 23

Every night that summer, you'd drag in after I was asleep. Sometimes I'd wake up and you'd be whispering nonsense in the dark. Talking about some chickababe named Phoenix like you was the Mad Hatter in <u>Alice in</u>

Wonderland. I don't know whether you was talking in your sleep or mind reading out loud. Had to pull the pillow over my head to shut out your jabberwocky.

When I opened my eyes one middle of the night in early August, I learnt what "scared stiff" really means. Something felt god-awful different. Like hot air pressing down. A shadow hung close to my face. I tried to get up but couldn't move. Tried to scream but my breath got stuck in my tonsils. Luckily I realized it was just you standing there before I learnt firsthand what "scared to death" means. I breathed.

"Ash! You scared the daylights out of me."

Ordinarily you'd of said something smart about NIGHT-lights, but you didn't say nothing, just turned away like a zombie and got into bed.

After that I had trouble sleeping. Lots of trouble.

January 24

Didn't sleep at all the night of my birthday, August 22, cause of you. Merle & me didn't talk to each other, not even one word, for a whole year to the day, BECAUSE OF YOU. What happened was

Forget it. I ain't in the mood.

January 25

Still ain't.

It's hard to sleep,
When you can't count sheep.

I was 5, you & Deena was in school, when a salesman come around trying to sell a vacuum cleaner so strong it would suck up all the dirt from UNDERNEATH the carpet. He had Mama run her vacuum in the living room, and then he run his right after her. The hose was see-through so we could watch all the crap come in that shoulda been in Mama's vacuum bag.

That didn't bother her—she said some people sweep dirt under the rug on purpose, and she didn't see why she needed to spend umpteen hundred $ to get rid of dirt nobody could see except in an industrial-strength see-through vacuum cleaner.

The salesman weren't about to be ushered out the door yet, though. Said the vacuum would also drag all the little sheep up out of bed mattresses.

"What sheep?" I says.

The guy looked serious at Mama. "You want your boy to know about this?"

"Whatever THIS is, it can't be any worse than what he'll imagine after you let sheep loose in his head," says Mama.

So he hauls a picture out of his pocket. Looks like an 8-legged monster sheep eating grass.

"These are dust mites," he says. "Microscopic insects that live on dead skin. Ashes to ashes and dust to dust. All dust is, is dead skin and—"

"I think that's enough definition," says Mama.

Well, after that I had to see the vacuum drag the sheep out of my mattress. The guy stripped my covers back and run the vacuum over the bed, and sure enough, dust swirled up the hose. A whole herd of microscopic sheep.

"Get that vacuum so the sheep won't eat my skin!" I says. Mama got rid of the salesman anyways. Then me & her got in the car and rode all the way to Sears in Bangor to buy plastic mattress covers to keep the sheep inside all the beds. When we got home, Mama dusted every inch of the house. Even over the doors & windows.

Counting sheep never put me to sleep after that.

Why Bed Ain't the Best Place to Be

Plenty of other scenes happened before my birthday anyways. I'll tell you about them 1st.

Life that summer weren't no fun, with Deena suffering from Teen Disease and you acting like the Libbys was the plague. I missed Merle something awful. The Daigles was living out to camp and only brung him into town for errands & church. Plus Merle discovered why they call male & female the opposite sex, as in let's you & me get on opposite sides of this dust mote and stare it down. Her name was Noel Lovell, no relation to Pudgy, lucky for Merle.

Don't laugh, but it got so I looked forward to getting the housework & campground cleaning done early so I could ride bike down to visit Grammy Ethyl on her lunch hour. It's easy to make fun of her narrating & interfering, but the truth is, after you been away from it awhile, you think happy thoughts about her. Like how much you'd love to be in her kitchen biting into a chunk of her homemade double-chocolate-marshmallow fudge with nuts. Or how nice it was of her to wink & slip you the $10 bill while Daddy was insisting that grandsons cat-sit for free. It gets so you CAN'T WAIT to see her again cause what you remember is how much she really loves you, not how much she gets on your nerves.

Lunch hour with Grammy Ethyl is just about right.

Course, just cause it weren't much fun don't mean the summer weren't lively.

You was gonna be starting college up the road at the

University of Maine at Machias in September. You coulda gone most anywheres, with your grades and talents, but Machias was the only place you could afford without loans.

"I'm not about to mortgage my life away," you'd say whenever anyone tsk-tsked you for wasting your music talent. The folks said you oughta be going to Juilliard or the University of Maine at Orono, not a college that churned out gym teachers.

Anyways, you was gonna live at home and drive to school in your new blue Chevy Nova. New to you—it had been around. So had the odometer, at least once. That car was older than you were. I'll never forget the midnight you zoomed into the driveway, honking the horn and yelling for the whole world to come see your new wheels. The doors to the units all smacked open like it was a fire drill. Well, all the doors that had tourists behind them. The clouds was busier than Libby's.

The honks & doors jolted me from dead sleep. On my way outa the house, I was on Daddy's heels—he was yanking up & buckling on his pants as he went.

Mama was already on the doorstep saying, "Ash! Cut it out!" A deep whisper that carried like a scream. Noises seemed louder than they would in sunshine. The night was muggy, starless.

Daddy run at you and just plain yelled some pungent English.

"Come on for a ride in my new wheels," you slurred. Between honks.

The customers all started in at once, and not "Why yes thank you, I'd love to take a little spin." It weren't easy to catch words, with everyone pitching them, but some like "money back" and "police" stuck out.

Mama give Daddy a MEANINGFUL STARE and headed off towards the units, saying, "It's all right, everything's under control now." Meanwhile, Daddy snatched you by the shirt neck and yanked you out of the driver's seat.

The honking stopped as you sailed to the tar. You landed on your rear and says, "What you think you're doing, dammit?" Jumped to your feet like a dog someone tickled too rough.

I watched Daddy in the dim light of the streetlamp. Little red spiders was coming out on his cheeks. His mouth was pinched shut. Hands, white knobs at his sides. The Mt. Rushmore look.

"If you don't want me to unbuckle my belt, you'll get your tail inside," Daddy finally growled at you. "NOW."

You locked a glare on him, and the both of you stared at each other, not a word, for a long time. I couldn't see Daddy's eyes, but he had to feel lousy. Your eyes was full of poison. Curdled my stomach.

Slowly Daddy's fists unfolded. Slowly he unbuckled his belt. Slowly he pulled it free of the 1st loop, the 2nd loop, the 3rd . . .

Still glaring at him, you hocked on the driveway. Then, without a syllable, you went inside.

"Well, Wesley," Daddy says. Sighing. Rethreading his belt. Quickly. "College will put an end to Ash's growing pains. Don't you think?" He put his hand on my shoulder and kneaded me like bread.

The look in his eyes was fear, the panicky kind kids get when they don't understand the directions on a test, they don't have one idea how to figure it out, and nobody'll explain.

"Sure, Daddy," I says. "Sure." But I weren't.

January 28

You & Deena & me always use to spend the last week of July up to Caribou with Grammy & Grampy Tibbetts. Who I'd rather be with than anyone (except Merle in the Shibboleth) (or you before the moose) cause they know their TV and don't speak much English except "More popcorn, honey? Ice cream? Mountain Dew?" But that summer there was lots of debate about whether or not we should go. I was on the WHETHER side, till you volunteered to drive us up there. The perfect way to break in your rusty new Nova.

Break down, more like. If you didn't break a moose first.

The idea of you driving switched me over to the OR NOT side real quick. Mama too. "Gee, Ash, that's awful nice of you," she says. "But you can't really afford to take all that time offen work this year. In fact"—she squinted at Deena—"maybe we should skip the visit to Grammy & Grampy's this year. Deena is—er—grounded."

That smelt like B.S. to me. Mama just didn't want to

be the one responsible for spreading Teen Disease all the way up to the Canadian border. The rate you was going, it wouldn't take long to turn "Tibbetts" into a swear word in Caribou. And if Deena could get into so much trouble right under Mama & Daddy's considerable nose, imagine all the fun she'd get into behind Grammy & Grampy's back.

I says, "That mean Ash & Deena ain't ALLOWED up to Grammy & Grampy's this summer?"

Deena's irises did a little polka for me. "Will wonders never cease. A spark of insight got past the brain damage."

Mama shook her head at Deena. "Watch the mouth." To me she says, "Yeah, I guess that's what it means."

"Oh shucks," says Deena. "And I been SO looking forward to being exiled for a week in Siberia." And she run to the phone.

If you wasn't driving and Deena wasn't going, then I was definitely back on the WHETHER side. "It ain't fair not to let ME go, Mama," I says. "Just think how disappointed your own dearly beloved folks'll be if they don't see their favorite youngest grandson this summer. They probably already laid in a whole case of Mountain Dew."

Daddy, who'd done a great job of keeping out of this one so far, finally come to the rescue. "Wes is right, Bonnie. He loves visiting your folks—you can't take that away from him. Besides, it would do him some good to get away from this place for awhile. Heck, I wish I could spend the week up there with him myself."

"I'LL drive him," says Mama.

You couldn't ask for better parents, now could you?

I don't know what messes you dragged home while I was up to Caribou, but I don't care. I was busy letting ice cream melt in my mouth.

January 29

The 2nd week of August, Daddy had to drive Grammy Ethyl out to Massachusetts for her sister's funeral. He weren't happy about it, and not just cause he loved Great-Auntie Mildred and hated Masshole drivers even more than Molasses and Maine-iacs. He was pretty nervous about leaving Libby's, with you & Deena acting like you was acting. So he temporarily ungrounded Deena and took her with him. She was THRILLED to spend 3 days away from The Hormone so she could say over Great-Auntie Mildred's casket, "Don't she look pretty! I ain't seen her look so young in 10 years. It's really a blessing, ain't it—she was just about all used up."

When Merle's mother heard about the death in the family, she invited me out to camp to help me take my mind offen my grief. If I'd of known it was gonna be my last overnight with Merle, I'd of paid better attention to all the fun I was having. But I didn't know, so all I remember is the grief Belinda caused me. Nagging me to nag you to make up with the Boys so the town would make up with you so she & Deena & the rest of the junior-going-on-senior partyers would stop getting the evil eye wherever they went. (Which weren't far.) She didn't know yet that you had more than your music act to get back together.

When Merle's mother dropped me off home the next day, the driveway was crammed with cars getting rained on, none of them ours. The house throbbed with live music, and the band weren't butchering Hank Williams Jr., neither—it was belting out rock & roll better than my breadbox. My heart was driving Maine-iac. Good old Ash old boy back with the Boys, new & improved, and the dastardly summer erased! So I thought.

I sprinted into the house and down cellar. I don't know if I noticed 1st that the family room stunk of beer & smoke or that it weren't the Upcountry Boys jamming. The music stopped soon's I opened the door, and I seen the backs of strangers bent over, not doing a very good job of hiding their bottles and ashtrays behind the couch. Smart to try, though—Mama wouldn't appreciate pot smoking in Libby's legal establishment. I known it was weed cause it smelt like Shawn "Reform School" Fox's jean jacket.

"Don't worry—it's just my man Wes," you says with a dumb grin. "C'mon in and listen to the Weather Forecasters."

Weather Forecasters, my toenail. THAT was the group you shoulda called the Knights of Sisyphus—they looked pretty useless. They looked pretty UGSOME. Since you didn't introduce them, I named them Devil-Shirt, Baldy & Abe-ette. Then there's you, Mr. All-

American Blond Blue Eyes in a pair of clean jeans and a new rugby shirt. Compared to them you was the nut in the box of raisins. All together I named you Ash & the Wackos.

Ash & the
Wackos

I set on the couch and listened awhile before it hit me that you was suppose to be at the blueberry factory.

Come to find out later—you was suppose to be tending office while Mama done some shopping, and she'd pay you for it cause you supposedly got LAID OFF at the factory. The blueberry crop was rotting in the rain, you says. Not enough work to go around. Up to church the next Sunday we overheard the truth. There was a bumper blueberry crop and you got FIRED cause you was taking naps in the warehouse. If you showed up to work at all.

Before Mama found out the facts, she felt sorry for you. Poor Ash, laid off and no $ coming in for college! So she found some excuse to leave and pay you to tend desk every afternoon when Daddy was gone to the funeral.

As soon as she left, & THE WACKOS arrived, and they'd be gone before she got back.

The band did play pretty good music. Weren't all hits & oldies, neither. You'd make stuff up as you went along—what's the word? IMPROVISE. The 1st day, you hit on a song so good that you made a demo tape to send to a recording studio. It was called "Maureen," and it went like this—Ash on melody, & the Wackos on ya-yas.

Maureen

There's such a thing as predestination,
>*ya ya ya ya*

It's a biological clock a racin',
>*ya ya ya ya*

God's got my biography writ in
>*oh oh ah ah*

Writ out on my DNA
>*DNA DNA*

In deoxyribonucleic acid
>*heredity is destiny*
>*my future is inside of me*
>*causes deja vu & prophecy*

Our days tick by gene by gene
And how I wish that I could read God's plan
To know if you're the one for me, Maureen!
>*ya ya oh oh ah ah DNA*
>>*Maureen*

Devil-Shirt wanted it to be about his girlfriend Michelle, but that didn't sound right with "gene" and "God's plan," so you settled for Michelle's sister Maureen.

Just cause the music was good didn't make it much fun having the band around, though. Nerve-WRECKing! What if the folks found out? They'd explode. Explode YOU. And maybe me too, if I was in the way.

January 30

The 2nd day, you stopped in the middle of making up your "signature" tune, "Cloudy with a Chance of Pain."

"Customer in the office, Wes," you says. "Take care of it for me, will you?"

There was 3 of them wanting to check in, and them days 3 was a crowd. I can't tell you how jittery it made me, them customers waiting. Mama'd apologize if they had to wait for her to take the cap offen her pen.

I decided to tend office.

The 3rd day, Mama come home early while the band was blasting "Maureen." I chased her down cellar to see what she'd do.

She yanked the cord out of your electric guitar. Then her hands was on her hips, and for once she forgot to turn the other cheek. "You stupid ass! You dumb, you idiotic, you STUPID—"

"Heeeeeyyy, Mumski, what's going down?" says Devil-Shirt. He never changed clothes.

Mama stared at him and shook her head like she had to jerk her brains into believing what she was seeing. Then she looked back at you.

"I thought you were watching the desk!"

"Until you barged in and messed me up," you says. Spit flying. "We didn't get any customers, for your information."

Mama squinted at you. "Say vray?" (Translation: say WHAT?!) "How do you expect to know when there's a customer if you're deafening yourself!"

"Oh, Mother," you says. Suddenly all calm and condescending. "You know very well that I can read minds. I got it from you. And there weren't any minds to read in the office since you left. Look right here—the amplifier's on the right frequency."

You plugged your guitar back in, then leaned towards the strings and strummed them gently. "See? No voices, no customers."

Actually we'd had 2 check-ins and a replacement-window salesman in the office. My throat wanted to choke out a laugh, but I choked it down and waited for a sign you was joking. No sign come. Your friends didn't look amused, just straight-faced like you was a science teacher.

"That's NOT funny, Ashton," Mama says.

Your forehead went to prunes. Mama'd offended you major. Then it hit me: you really did mean what you said. Hit Mama too, like the Blazer hit the moose.

"Oh, good Lord." Mama's face turned GRAY.

Your friends just looked bored.

"C'mon, man, let's split," says Baldy. You nodded, and the group took off in the Ash breeze.

"Hey, you get your butts back here & clean up this mess," Mama yelled after you. But you didn't.

"Wes, you don't have to pick up after them," she says. "Just leave this stuff here for Ash." I didn't tell her I'd already picked up after you 2 days. That day I left the beer bottles & pot-trays. Left them the next day too, and the next, till finally Mama give in and picked up after you herself.

Soon's you & the Wackos left, Mama went for a long walk back & forth in front of the kitchen door waiting for Daddy to get home from Massachusetts. She didn't even give him a chance to complain about Mass-hole drivers—she says, "Steve, Ash is on drugs."

"Huh?" Daddy frowned, flashed a double take at me. "Bonnie, this is hardly the—"

"Wes knows all about it. Probably seen more in one day than—"

"Knows? Seen? What you talking about?" Daddy took Mama's arm and led her to the sitting couch.

"What happened?" says Deena.

"You keep your mouth out of this," snapped Mama. All nerved up. "Steve, Ash is . . . I don't know, hallucinating or something. Acting strange." And she told what happened.

Daddy had a few minutes of drill-sergeant face while he listened. "I oughta throw the book at him. I oughta throw him out of the house, is what I oughta throw!"

Mama says, "If it's really drugs, he doesn't need the boot. He needs help."

"You should still do <u>some</u> ASH-kicking, though," says Deena.

Daddy ignored that and leaned over to squeeze Mama's shoulders. Now he spoke hushed, "At least now we know what ails that kid, and we can get him squared away. We'll be alrite, Bonnie."

Mama took a deep breath, jumped up, and run to her room. As she passed the wall mirror I seen her face. Scrunched like one of them apple dolls we use to make in art class for Halloween.

Mama don't hardly ever cry, but she weren't going to her room to iron shirts.

January 31

That night Mama & Daddy set in the living room waiting up for you. They wouldn't let me keep them company. "Thanks but no thanks—go to bed." I stared up at the shadows on the ceiling. Listened to the TV mumble. Couldn't sleep with the biggest fight in the history of the Libbys ready to go down. (Biggest up till then.) Last time I looked at the clock it was 2 A.M. Then suddenly Mama was shaking me awake. My head felt like a used bandage. Out of the little bit of eye I could crack open, I seen the clock numbers flip to 11:00. You was flopped across your

79

bed, sound asleep with your arms straight out to the sides & your ankles crossed.

So I missed the explosion. I groaned. This tired body, and I didn't get nothing for it.

"I'm staying in bed today," I says.

"You dying? You got chicken pox?"

"Been exposed to kryptonite. Can't get up."

"If I can, you can," she says. "We got a family meeting in 5 minutes." And suddenly my derriere (61 Scrabble points for Krista, long ago) was getting some air.

Then it was your turn. You'd went to sleep in your clothes, on top of the bedspread. So Mama couldn't give you the cold kiss of morning. She tossed you, she turned you, but she couldn't wake you up.

"Must be exhausted from last night." Mama shook her head.

I yawned on my way to the bureau. "What happened?"

"Nothing happened." I couldn't hardly hear her whisper. "Your father & I fell asleep on the couch after the national anthem." Even though that couch is for sitting. I was gonna tell her the satellite dish does get stations that never fuzz off for the night, but the way she was looking at you froze my tongue.

Her look pulled at my heart in a way I could never explain right. Wicked sad. I had to look away or hug her. Somehow I known which one she could use. And I'll admit here since nobody else will ever see this, especially not Merle R. Daigle, it felt good to me too.

We started the family meeting <u>about</u> you <u>without</u> you.

"If he admits to taking drugs, then he'll have to stop," Mama announced. "Once the facts are known, only a fool would use drugs. <u>Saw-tayed</u> brains." (She meant fried.) "Ash is nobody's fool."

Deena coughed. I was sure she was clearing the way for one of them ASH bASHes she learnt by heart so they'd pop out at the right moment. But she just said, "What facts is they?"

"These facts." Mama slapped a fat envelope onto the kitchen table. "I just got this information at the library. When he reads this, Ash'll flush his drugs down the hopper and say <u>pardonay-mwah</u> to the wrong crowd he's got into."

Daddy pulled a pile of photocopies outa the envelope. "The result of marijuana and other drugs on young people is often a loss of maturing experience that deprives them of growth and leads to—"

"You must be joking, Mama." Deena sounded like a horse with a bellyache. "You think Ash is gonna read this propaganda? After 1/2 a sentence he'll be out the door."

Mama sighed a few times before words come out. "I know that's a chance we take. But we have to try. Whenever you can slip it into the conversation, mention what you know about how dangerous drugs are and how they change people. The message's gotta sink in."

I ain't much for MESSAGES myself. And I known

you wasn't neither. But I didn't know what else we could do. They sent Shawn Fox to reform school, but they couldn't make him REFORM. You was 18, old enough to do what you wanted. Mama & Daddy was powerless. If they ordered me to read a ream of photocopies, I'd have to. But they couldn't make you do nothing. You could up and move out.

Part of me wished you would. I didn't like sleeping in the same room with you. But if you left home, how would we ever know what trouble you was in?

The clock radio in our room blared on and then went quiet.

"Remember, Steve," says Mama, tapping <u>How to Protect Your Scout from Drug Abuse: A Parent's Guide,</u> "discuss the problem with the child in a calm, objective manner."

Before Daddy could answer, you limped into the kitchen. You looked more than beat. You looked beat UP.

Mama says, "Morning Ash. Get yourself a cup of coffee & have a seat."

Deena cleared her throat and held up the envelope. "We got some fascinating reading material here for your enjoyment."

Mama slapped at Deena's leg like it had a mosquito on it.

You leaned against the door frame and stared out the window at the cardinals in Deena's shrubs. "I'm awful stiff today." Words stiff too.

"Ayuh," says Mama. We all known in our ligaments just how you felt.

Daddy pet your chair. "Well, #1 son. Take a load off. We got some talking to do."

You was smiling this pained, knowing smile, same as Mrs. Pike telling Daddy it's nice to see him in church again this year. "Awful stiff & sore," you says. "Spent the night nailed on the cross."

You lit a cigarette and, with it hanging between your lips, sloshed coffee into a mug. That's how I noticed your hands. Curled stiff, like they hurt. Them drugs must cause some god-awful nightmares, I'm thinking.

You took a sip and winced like your lips was raw. Without another word, you limped out the front door slow, careful.

"Jesus Christ," Deena mumbled.

It weren't swearing. We all known what she meant.

The shock wore off Daddy enough to yell out the door, "Where you think you're going, Ashton! Get your ass back here!" But the rusty blue Nova was already pulling out.

February 2

Mama weren't about to let you turn around in that house without facing her & her message. Her most ingenious idea was to hide the toilet paper roll under a paperback book, <u>Drugs and Kids.</u>

"Don't forget to put <u>Drugs and Kids</u> back when

you're done," she'd yell every time Deena or me flushed. Since it was the only reading material allowed in the can, we got so we could quote the good parts, like "Families and friends of abusers often suffer a great deal" and "Addiction is a 3-headed dragon you have to behead—physical, psychological & spiritual."

"You don't mean to tell me one of our kids is on drugs, do you?" says Grammy Ethyl one day after she spent some time on the throne.

"Right Ethyl," says Mama real fast, "I don't mean to tell you that at all."

We wasn't suppose to tell NOBODY about your little problem.

"That book you seen's just a research project," says Deena. "Did you know that Narragansett contains a chemical substance called ETHYL ALCOHOL?"

Them days seeing you was like seeing a ghost. You was a rare sight, and when we spoke to you, you either flit out of the house or just ignored us like we wasn't there. "As the use of a sedative-hypnotic drug becomes habitual, the difference in dosage between becoming high and becoming dead becomes minuscule," says Deena.

However, it was easy to see you'd BEEN there. Instead of Mr. Clean, Mr. 3 Baths a Day, you was turning into Mr. B.O., Mr. Cigarette Butts on the Floor. Which made me ugly, considering how I earnt my allowance. One night when I went to bed my covers was a rat's nest that smelt like your shit, which is the only correct term for it, and explains why you didn't seem to be getting the message on top of the toilet paper. Just thinking about it makes me want to rip sheets. I run all over the house to find you and pound on you, but you was long flit out.

Me & Mama was making blueberry Danish one morning, and you suddenly was there watching her. "I'm glad you're here, Ash. Sit, let's talk," Mama says. You didn't sit, didn't talk, just kept watching her, but not like a zombie. More like you was looking for something under a microscope. That look tied my gut into about 40-11 knots, and I weren't even the specimen.

"Ash, we need to talk about drugs." Sweat popping out over Mama's lip. Voice getting higher.

You stared on.

"Don't deny it—we already know. We want to help you, but we can't until you talk."

And on.

"Talk, goddamyou!" Mama, swearing in ENGLISH? A nervous wreck.

You stared another few seconds till the corners of your mouth tilted up in the spookiest smile I ever seen— Mona Lisa without the sugar. Like you found a secret you was looking for, and it made you smug.

February 3

Okay, I know what you'll say, "Wes, Wes, Wes, don't hold a grudge, let bygones be bygones. You & Merle made up, didn't you?" Except Merle and me ain't the SAME, Ash.

We're speaking now, and he's still my best friend, but I ain't his. He wouldn't say so to me, but I know he'd rather be with Noel Lovell anytime. They was like Siamese twins the whole year Merle & me wasn't speaking. I know Noel can be FRIENDS in a way I can't, but it ain't just that. Merle hangs out with the basketball bozos now. He's good enough to start, but he flubs up on purpose so he can watch Noel's pom-poms from the bench. He didn't go out for basketball—he went out for bus rides home from away games.

Cheerleaders do have impressive talent—they can appear to be in their seat up front when they're really down back in their boyfriend's lap.

Anyways, not that I expected you to show up or nothing, but on one of your flits into the house I invited you to come to my birthday party. Play guitar, sing if you wanted to. Mess around by the pool. It weren't no big deal, just us Libbys, Grammy Ethyl, and all the Daigles on a Saturday afternoon. I invited Merle's folks to entertain Mama & Daddy—Merle & I had a major hard time to give Belinda & Deena. Girls always practically ASK for it, anyways. That day they was lying on their stomachs with their bikini tops unhooked so they wouldn't get untan lines. It was hot for once. August 22, and summer finally got to Maine. So there was quite a few customers there too.

Okay, there me & Merle was, floating on air mattresses in the pool, drinking Coke out of champagne glasses, putting our ice-cream bowls on the girls' bare backs, yanking their bikini strings—having a blast celebrating my big ONE FOUR—when along you come singing "Happy Birthday" like the emperor in his new clothes. Nothing on but your electric guitar. Hauling the amplifier behind you in a little red wagon. Extension cord dragging behind that.

Nobody said, "Hold on to your hat."

"You should be ASHamed of yourself!" says Deena.

"Keep it covered, Ash," growled Daddy, "and get yourself back inside right now." Giving you the Mt. Rushmore look. His knob-fists unfolded and reached for his belt, but he was wearing trunks.

You looked square at Merle and says, "Merle doesn't think I know this, but he wants to—"

No, I can't write that! I can't even stand thinking the word you says he wanted to do to Belinda. His sister! And THEN you says he only wanted to do that to his sister cause he couldn't do it to his mother, even though his mother didn't like what she got from his father.

Daddy was after you in a flash. This time he didn't have no belt loops or shirt neck to haul you off by. He just plain shoved you, hard, 3 times, till your back was against the fence. He held you there with one hand as the other hand whipped back.

"Go ahead," you says. "Scapegoat the messenger. It won't be the first time in history."

The hand started down.

Mama was up and running. "Steve! Don't play with matches!" Seemed like a funny thing to say at the moment, but it meant something to Daddy cause his punching arm went limp and his head snapped around. He kept his other hand on your chest as he looked at Mama.

"Bonnie, this time he's gone too far."

"If you don't, I will," says Mr. Daigle, on his feet, his fist up.

Daddy made a fist at Mr. Daigle. "You mind your own business. This is my boy, and I'll take care of him."

Mama pushed on Daddy's arm. "Whatever you do, take it inside!"

In a flash, Daddy had you shoved into the office. The door slammed behind you.

At that, everyone on the deck started into each other, so I couldn't hear whether or not Daddy give it to you good. There was customers demanding a free night cause the scene spoilt their one fair-weather vacation day. And there was Daigles demanding apologies.

Grammy was setting there shocked quiet for the 1st time in my life.

Merle told me he always thought you was an asshole too big for your britches anyways. I told Merle he was a liar cause he use to worship you the same's I did, and if he didn't have the sense to see there was something wrong and you wasn't yourself, then maybe he had an IQ problem or a loyalty problem and either way he had a best friend problem.

I honestly forget the rest. It was one of them stupid arguments when you throw around all the little grudges you ever held in, or make up new ones, just so the other

person won't think he won. At the same time, Deena &
Belinda and Mama & Mrs. Daigle was dancing around
the same ring—all trying for a knockout. Them words we
thrown at each other hurt worse than punches. As soon
as Merle finished saying, "Oh yeah, well you're an igno-
rant stuttering thief," his mother told him to get in the
car and never set foot on low-life Libby property again.

Deena & Belinda was on the phone again in a week.
I didn't even need to write Merle a letter to rip up the
hate—I woulda made up with him the next minute if he'd
of talked to me. But when I got to the Shibboleth the
next day, he'd hung a sheet down the middle to keep me
offen his 1/2, and that was his last word to me for a year.
It's been almost a year and a 1/2, and Mama & Mrs.
Daigle still ain't speaking. Ash, you should see Mama
glance over to the Daigles' pew in church. Use to be mad
and hurt in her eyes. "Lila Daigle, how dare you say that."
But now there's just sorry and wish. "I'm so sorry—I wish
it never happened."

I know the feeling. Sometimes I'm sorry I gotta put
you through the stuff in this book. Even though every
word is the truth you already put me through. Holy Bat-
mobile, I wish it never happened.

February 4

All the night of my birthday and all Sunday, the folks,
Deena & me kept watch for you. Daddy alone when it
was time for church. It was hot, but we locked the win-

dows anyways and slide-bolted the cellar & office doors so you'd have to come in the front. At night we took guard shifts so everyone could lay down for awhile. Maybe Deena slept, not me.

When we caught you, Daddy was gonna give you the old "get help or get out" talk. But we never caught you, even though there was signs you'd been in the room. Cigarette ashes all over. Dirty clothes on the floor. (Don't ask me when you took them off. Or put them ON.)

"That's it—I've had it," Mama says. And the next night she camped out in our room. On a stack of quilts the other side of your bed so she'd see you before you seen her.

Deena had to help lay down the quilts. "This is a waste of time," she says. A waste of Deena's heavy-breathing-over-the-phone time, I was thinking. Then her smart mouth goes, "I bet the son of God don't come home at all."

Mama's hand snapped back. Deena looked away. I closed my eyes and held my breath for the slap. But what I heard was both of them busting into tears and "I'm sorry." You had our nerves to going like spit on an iron.

Funny, it didn't take long to get to sleep that night with Mama over in the corner between your bed and the wall. But the next thing I known, the room felt like the gym during a basketball game, all rocking loud.

You.

Only this time, it weren't your music. It was you &

Mama yelling. I jumped up to snap the lights on and seen her setting on top of you on your bed. She had you pinned down like a TV wrastler, your arms crossed behind your head. You was struggling something fierce but couldn't get away cause Mama had you tucked in.

When the lights blared on, the both of you squinted and looked at me for an instant. Then you went right back at it.

MAMA: "Sit still, you—I just wanna talk!"
ASH: "Mother, you raving maniac, get offen me before I have to hurt you!"
MAMA: "You're the son of Bonnie Libby, and you're gonna listen to me!"
ASH: "Get your ass off, or I'll—"
DADDY: (From doorway.) "YOU'LL WHAT!"

The air whooshed by my face as he run to take Mama's place setting on you and pinning your arms back. "Ashton Libby you simmer down or I'll, I'll—"

"I know, I know," you says, "or you'll beat the shit outa me. Tell the truth. You've always hated me, haven't you, old man?"

Daddy shook his head. His expression made an about-face. Sad wiped out the anger. Then out come the gentlest voice I ever heard from him, "No, son. Don't you know? You're my boy. I love you."

And like a miracle, all the hate and anger melted offen your face too. With them gone, we could see the fear in you, all white and wobbly. Your mouth crumpled, and you whimpered in a way nobody can help. Like stomping barefoot on a nail you didn't see.

"Your move, cow," you whispered.

Mama's face went soft—it was almost smiling. I seen that look once before. Her salvation face. The Sunday I went up to the front of the church and accepted Jesus as my savior.

She tipped her head at me. "Why don't you sleep on the couch downstair?" She kissed my cheek, and I left. Glad to.

Nobody ever told me what went on in that room that night, but you was home in the morning, and you called the family into the bathroom to watch you flush your weed & speed down the toilet.

February 5

You wasn't quite your old fun self, but you was with the family, and that felt good. We all wanted things hunky-dory, so that's what they was. You was home, the Wackos wasn't, and that was enough.

My foot.

February 6

You started at college, and over the next few weeks I could tell you was trying real hard to act normal. Most of the time you was at the kitchen table with your college books spread out. Studying, you says. But you was doing more muttering to yourself than reading or writing. When Mama or Daddy was in the room, they'd say, "Talking to me, Ash?" and you'd say, "Just studying" and keep quiet till they left.

I known it weren't "studying" cause you wasn't muttering about mitochondria or organelles or them other too-long-for-Scrabble words in your fat biology book. You wasn't even muttering about the Fundamentals of Speech Communication.

Listening to you was like eavesdropping on one end of a telephone conversation. I'd only catch 1/2 the discussion. And your 1/2 was wicked weird.

"Good one, Mr. Codfish." You'd smile and laugh to yourself.

"I told you to be quiet and let me study, you pompous Jude-ass." A dirty look.

Good thing Grammy Ethyl weren't actually around to hear it when you asked her if she realized she was an aardvark in a former life.

And more. Lots more.

One time when you WAS reading a book, you jerked your head up, looked all around the kitchen, then asked me, "What was that Mama said?"

"What? When?" I says.

"Just now—you heard her. It's torture. She sneaks around and whispers in my ear, then hides. She resents me for giving her stretch marks so she couldn't pose for Playboy."

It weren't the right time to laugh, but I couldn't help it and I couldn't hardly stop. It ain't funny thinking about your mother in a girlie magazine—it's sicko. Finally I says, "Ash, you're hearing things. Mama left for the grocery store 1/2 an hour ago."

You shook your head sad, like I disappointed you. "Don't let her brainwash you, Wes."

Stuff like that was why I got in the habit of sleeping on the couch downstair.

February 7

One day when me & Deena got offen the school bus, you was sitting IN the window over your bed, filling it with legs and guitar. Good old-fashioned unelectric guitar strings strumming, starting & stopping with your voice, the way you use to practice a new song or make one up.

"Talk about a pane," says Deena behind me. "When's the last time you washed your window, Wes? It's plastered with ASH."

You was singing. "Wes old boy, hows about some harmonizing?" Deena laughed, maybe at her rapier wit, or maybe she heard harmony expected of me, which is something Miss Small would call "irony."

My violin was waiting on my bed when I got in the room.

"My foot," I says.

"Come on, Wes. Practice makes closer to perfect. And playing by yourself in the bathroom is doing diddly-squat for your ear. You gotta harmonize, brother."

The shine in your eyes suckered me into thinking I really could. I picked up the violin and screeched a warm-up scale.

"Wes Wes Wes, you ain't scraping carrots with that bow! Make it one with your body. See, my pick is my fingernail." You strum, and hum, and it is one sound.

I scraped another carrot.

You shook your head. "No no no. It's like leaning into a curve when you're driving the Arctic Cat. See, my guitar is my body." Then you strummed this melody, Ash, and hummed, and out come the most beautiful song I ever heard you sing. Well, I mean your voice & the melody was beautiful. Like a hymn. The words ain't pretty, so far as I can tell—I don't get them. You had me write them down so they'd become part of my body and I could play the song on violin.

Voice of the Phoenix
I listened this morning into the sun
And found warmth that opens buds, brightens
* skies,*
Brings droughts to fields and blinds man's eyes.
* This is the voice of the Phoenix.*
I listened this evening into the moon
And found no warmth, no fire inside

Of the rock that pulls on mood and tide.
This is the voice of the Phoenix.
I've listened all day to the fly and the spider
Discussing ancestors who lived together
In a lost garden with no need for a web.
This is the voice of the Phoenix.
I've listened all my life to the chickadee
Singing can't you see how to be-be-be.
It is written in every rock and tree.
This is the voice of the Phoenix.

"Lean right into it with your soul," you says, and nodded at me to try.

I put the violin to my cheek and lifted the bow, but I couldn't play. Not in your air. I was thinking your music is your soul, and it's still floating around the room on them little dust specks that light up in a sunbeam. Pieces of the brother I use to know. Did them drugs you was quitting make your soul peel off like dead skin?

If I looked at you or talked, I'd cry. Took off for the bathroom, locked the door, and leaned into the violin. Scraped my guts out.

February 8

The Sunday after my birthday, Merle was already attached to Noel Lovell at the head, by the looks of them in church. She never use to go there—I figured Merle musta SAVED her. Anyways, there weren't no line waiting for his spot in my pew.

Enough of setting out in my 1/2 of the Shibboleth listening to Merle turn his comic book pages, praying that Jesus would move Merle to rip down that sheet and grin at me. I decided to make September Wes Libby Month. Flood the house with Friends of Wesley for once. I could make plenty at school if I wanted. We have a pool.

Then I changed my mind. Me & Merle go way back. We got the Shibboleth, we got Bible verses, we got private documents in our school lockers. We got memories like you saving our lives, and other secrets that I won't even put in this book. If I couldn't have Merle, I didn't want no friends. Cause if a friend like him ain't forever, what's gonna make someone else any better?

It was the same with Daddy & Pastor Lovell, I think. Daddy hardly ever mentioned the couples him & Mama hung out with, but he was always telling funny stories about him & Pudgy growing up, him & Pudgy in the military, him & Pudgy at the factory. Daddy coulda told Grammy Ethyl to stop plaguing him about Pastor Pudgy, but he never did. Cause deep down in his heart there was a soft spot with Bradley Lovell's name on it, and he didn't want that spot hardening into a gravestone.

But you probably won't understand this, Ash—you never had a best friend. When people use to ask, "Who's your best friend, Ash?" you'd say, "I like ALL my friends."

There was enough in you for all of them, back then. Where are all your best friends now?

February 9

Guess I been what Miss Small would call DIGRESSING. I better just write down what happened before I run outa pages. The book's over 1/2 filled now, but the story ain't 1/2 over.

You was moving slower and slower. Like one of them TV commercial toys loaded with the OTHER batteries. Sometimes you'd set in the same spot for an hour without hardly moving. Awake, though. Maybe you'd blink. Maybe that edge-of-the-mouth smile'd creep onto your face. Creep_Y_, that smile. Since you still wasn't your old self, everyone thought you was having trouble getting offen drugs.

"I'm clean—cross my heart and hope to die," you says.

"You just crossed your heart to get away with lying," says Deena.

One day in late October when you was gone up to college, Krista brung over a friend of hers who was majoring in social work. They explained this idea called "intervention." Wanted us to "intervene" so you'd get yourself down to the state hospital rehab ward and dry out. The plan was, we'd each write you a letter about how your drugs had changed you and hurt us. The 1st line had to say, "I love you, Ash, and that's why I have to confront you with the truth." We'd all get together with you to read the letters out loud. Then you'd supposedly ASK to get in the Blazer with Mama & Daddy and drive down to the state hospital.

"That's the best stupid idea I ever heard," says Daddy. "Besides, English weren't exactly my best subject."

I forgot to tell you before—there's another reason I like to rip up them letters I write. I take after Daddy. But he already covered that excuse, so I says, "Ash will just ignore us or flit off."

"Or say the Archbishop of Canterbury put us up to it," says Deena. And she weren't hardly around to hear your malarkey cause she spent her free time up to the cafeteria practicing how to look foolish wagging her pom-poms in front of The Hormone warming bench at basketball games. (I'm sure she was more talented on the bus than she was in the gym.)

The social-work major said intervention usually turned out good with alcoholics, and alcohol's a drug, so it oughta turn out good with you, whatever you was taking.

Mama says, "It can't hurt to try."

Daddy says, "Oh, alrite. But I don't want no one seeing my i's and t's."

So we all writ you a letter. Even Grammy Ethyl. Mine was 10 pages. How you hit the moose and give me a concussion. Scratched my breadbox. Ruint my perfectly good sleep on misc. occasions. Also ruint my summer & my idea of you & my friendship with Merle, etc. etc. etc. Felt good & bad getting the dirt cleaned out from behind my ears and onto paper where I could see it. Like the dry itch after a nice hot shower—each scratch spreads the itch out worse. It got so thinking about you was one big itch between my shoulder blades, till I finally got up in the middle of the night on New Year's and started scratching this book to you. Leading up to THAT night. Guess in a few pages I'll REALLY be getting at that itch.

We had our intervention get-together a couple days before Halloween. Krista's the type to go 1st and get it over with, and Deena is too, so they fought over who would. Krista won. Her letter was full of messy stuff I never suspected. Like catching you with your pants down around Abe-ette, the little drummer girl from the Weather Forecasters. Only Krista known you was so high at the time that you didn't know what you was doing, and she loved you too much not to forgive you this once.

Deena's was even worse—she caught you trying to do unmentionables to her in the middle of the night. Left Grammy speechless for the 2nd time. Krista crying. Daddy saying, "No no no" under his breath, fingers tap-dancing on his belt buckle. Mama's face dry-apple scrunched, arm crawling around Deena's shoulders, squeezing, while Deena looked up to see how you took the unmentionables.

You was setting quiet on the couch with your eyes shut, like the girls was reading bedtime stories.

"I don't believe this," says Deena.

"Ashton! Wake up!" says Krista.

You didn't move, though.

"If he's gonna crASH, I ain't intervening," says Deena.

You didn't even twitch.

"It don't seem to be working," says Daddy.

"It certainly doesn't. I give up," says Krista, real meaningful, like it weren't just the intervention she give up on—it was YOU. And she left.

Deena went to her room, Daddy to the office, Mama to the kitchen. She was doing lots of baking them days to sell at the Trading Post so we'd have enough $ to get through the winter. Daddy was even talking about going back to work at the factory for awhile. Whatever shift Pudgy Lovell weren't on. Pudgy's a foreman there now. He has to keep his paying job cause he won't take a penny for doing the Lord's work (except gas $ so he can take Jesus to shut-ins).

I volunteered to take some time offen violin lessons to save $, but the folks wouldn't hear of it. So I was on my way to the bathroom with my violin when I seen you get up from the couch. There weren't no expression at all on your face. But there was a tear dribbling down your cheek. You moved slow, like a fly in the cold. Got your books from the table. Left.

You didn't come home that night. Mama & Daddy was some worried, back & forth like a couple of zoo cats. They didn't say nothing when Deena asked if Kenneth could come over and watch TV. When The Hormone got there the 2 of them flew to the family room. If Mama & Daddy realized this, they woulda paced right downstair lickety-split. But they was too busy looking out the window for a rusty blue Nova.

You didn't come home the next day neither. Come 3 A.M., Daddy started making calls. I was suppose to be asleep, but who could sleep in a house where nerves was like carpet shock in your fingertips. Mama jumped if anyone touched her.

Daddy called the hospital. No Ash. He called all your old friends from high school. No Ash, and the parents of all your old friends from high school weren't too pleased to get a phone call after 3 A.M. Daddy said "Sorry sorry sorry" more times in that 1/2 hour than I ever heard him say all added up.

Finally Daddy called the police station. "I want to report a missing son. 18. Yes, he lives at home. No, not just tonight. Didn't come home last night, neither. Well, yes, I guess you could say he likes to party, but what difference does that—"

I held my breath during the long silence.

"What's he saying?" Mama says.

"Alrite. Okay. I'll be in to file the forms in the

morning. Right, IF he don't come home. Thank you, offi-
cer."

The click of the phone hanging up seemed awful loud.

February 11

Next morning Mama had to shake me awake for school.
You still wasn't back.

DADDY: (Pacing the kitchen.) "We ain't gonna set
around waiting for him to come home in a body bag.
Bonnie, you and me're going looking for Ash. We'll check
out the police station and then ask around up at the
campus."
MAMA: "What about the customers?"
DADDY: "My mother—no, better keep her out of it.
Deena can stay home and tend the motor lodge."
DEENA: "ALRITE!!!!!"

I can't believe Mama & Daddy wasn't suspicious at
them exclamation points in Deena's voice. She LOVED
school. Mama & Daddy couldn't pry her offen The Hormone in the dark corners up to Narragansett High.

WES: "Now Daddy, you wouldn't want Deena to miss her
algebra test today—I'll watch the office and ream out the
rooms."
MAMA: (Shaking her head.) "You're too young, Wes. A
whole day with no adult around—it's too much responsi-

bility. Besides, it wouldn't look right to the customers during school hours."
WES: "I'll look uptown, then. Let me help."
DEENA: "He COULD stay home and help ME. . . ."

Help, my foot. She'd be setting behind the desk in front of a mirror waiting for The Hormone to skip out of school while I was scrubbing tubs. I thought of soap scum as I looked at her.

DADDY: (Exasperated.) "Wes, I know you're worried about your brother, but the best place for you right now is school. So get a move on before you miss the bus. Deena can handle Libby's (Long pause to lift eyebrows at her.) ALONE. Wes, I'll let you know the minute we find Ash. Deal?"
WES: "The minute?"
DADDY: "The minute."

I shook hands, but I weren't happy.
It weren't till I got on the bus and seen the driver in a gorilla suit that I remembered it was me & Merle's favorite holiday, Trick-or-Treat. (USE TO be our favorite.) That was the 1st time we didn't plan our costumes a month ahead. We always hit the streets at dusk and didn't head home till our grocery bags was packed. Which takes awhile in Calvin Cove.
That day at school I made a discovery—you can actually see a minute hand moving.

Nobody let me know a thing all day, so I figured you was still missing. At least that's what I figured till the bus crawled up the hill towards Libby's. The driveway coulda been a used-car lot. All them cars meant something happened. Maybe something awful. Like the day Grampy died. My guts felt like a bagful of pretzels.

None of the cars was ours, and the minute I got offen the bus I known why. The rock music was practically rolling the house over.

Ash & the Wackos was blasting in the basement.

The kitchen door was locked, so I run to the motel office. There was a clump of people standing there, but no Deena.

"Ain't you one of the owner's kids?" a man growled. Loud, over the music.

"We wanna talk to the owner," growled another guy. He had a streaky red face and one of them ball bellies a shirt hikes up over. The whites of his pockets eared out.

Mama & Daddy obviously wasn't there. Deena weren't there. And if you was ALL there, Ash, I wouldn't of been in the office feeling like the main dish at a cannibal banquet. "I'm the only one here," I wanted to say, but "Aah . . . aah . . . aah" was as close as I could get.

"Now Dougie. Don't get yourself all worked up," says a woman next to Ball Belly. "Your blood pressure!"

"I'll raise someone's blood pressure if that noise don't cut it right now. We been waiting years for this vacation, and I'll be damned if I'll spend it like this." Guess he didn't know Halloween ain't Vacationland season. Past pretty leaves, before snow sports.

This is what I thought: if I was smart, a quick thinker like Mama or you Ash, I'd know what to do. I'd say real smooth, "Don't worry, sir—the problem's being taken care of." Then I'd . . . what? See, I ain't any kind of thinker. I STILL ain't thought of nothing I coulda done.

The customers' voices all come pounding at me.

"Well, boy, you gonna straighten this out?"

"Lay off—he's just a kid."

"What kind of place is this with no adult around to do business?"

"I been waiting 1/2 an hour to check in. Guess I'll just keep driving till I find a place that WANTS my business."

"We're checking OUT. And tell your parents they better not have the gall to charge our credit card, or they'll hear from our lawyer!"

The week's meat money and my chance for new sneakers stomped off. I slumped down on the desk chair and stared at the holey hand-me-downs I was wearing till Mama's pie profits added up to a new pair. My feet felt the floor quiver with the music. The shoelaces actually waved at me.

I hoped it was a nightmare. Ridiculous, HOPING for a NIGHTMARE! But it weren't one. Even though I was a guy and 14, I wanted to cry. Stuck my fingers in my ears and set there instead, in case any more customers come in.

You'll have to wait for the rest—my writing fist's got cramps.

February 12

This is what you was playing over & over & over. Which is why I remember it. Wish it was as easy to forget.

Headlines

Over 60 cats found dying
Women in pond murdered, officials say
Old women face years of poverty
Family spats prompt 1000s to run away
Rape victim ignored by neighbors
Parents leave daughter on highway
Tot's death is charged to mother
Grandpa collecting for blind,
    DA didn't see it that way
Phony cop held in murder
Pretty girl tries suicide
Newborn girl found alive in trash heap
Search continues, man believes son died
Man tries suicide after committing homicide
Back at 1200 pounds, Walter Hudson dies
Imprisoned artist works behind bars
You can judge the book of life
    by the headlines

The digital clock in the office didn't have no hands, so I watched the seconds   blink   blink   blink   blink   blink   blink   till the beat and the blinks made my head woozy. It was like the worst hour of the stomach flu, when you think it won't never stop, you wish you could go to sleep and wake up normal, but the thing just won't give you no peace.

I was ready to scream. A wide-open animal scream. But first the office door opened. It was long-lost Deena, her hair all mussed and her face raw pink like sunburn. The Hormone needed a shave.

"Oh jeez," she says, all out of breath. "What's going on around here? The house has VIBRATO!"

"What, you get up on the wrong side of The Hormone's backseat today?" I says. Dumb, I know. Deena glared at me and burst through the door to the house just as the folks burst through the door to the office.

"What's going on here, Wes?" yelled Daddy. As if it could be anything but Ash & the Wackos.

"Trick or treat," I says.

Mama & Daddy looked at each other and run down cellar. I run after them.

You couldn't of found a seat or standing room even if you was an anorexic midget. Fans of Ash & the Wackos, wall to wall. Girls with long greasy hair, guys with long greasy hair, guys with no hair, girls with crew cuts—somebody even had green hair. Practically all I could see was their hair cause they was all packed together like food in the freezer. Backs to the door, faces to the band. I couldn't see you.

The place reeked of pot smoke. And Narragansett.

Deena was jumping up & down in the doorway, screeching full blast: "ASH! STOP! ASH! HEY, CLEAR OUT OF HERE, YOU CRACKPOTHEADS! PARTY'S OVER! JEEZ, MY PARENTS ARE GONNA KILL ME!"

Didn't do no good.

Mama went into the utility room, and suddenly the lights went out. Electricity stopped thrumming through the floor. Mama'd yanked the power to the basement. The only noise was the drum pounding and people singing. Hard to believe a drum beating, 3 unplugged guitars, and 4 people belting out a song could sound quiet, but they did compared to all the miked-up blinko. All the hairy & bald & green heads turned towards the door. The band music fluttered to nothing.

DADDY: "Atten-HUT! The party is now over! Get the hell OUTA HERE!"

His voice was a machine gun going off, but nobody budged.

MAMA: "Guess we'd better call the cops after all, Steve."

That done it, even though her voice was real calm. But I was beside her—I seen her neck veins popping out as the crowd grumbled past us. Took awhile for the room to clear, and finally I seen you setting on a beer keg, staring up and out one of them skinny cellar windows that lay on their side. Staring straight into the sun, it looked like. The rest of the Wackos stood there staring at you, waiting for a signal.

MAMA: (Into her fist.) "Mon Dyuh! The rug!"

Green carpet gone brown. Blackish-gray ash spots. Use to look shaggy like a dog. Now just mangy. When I stepped into the room, the carpet squished.

DEENA: "The cellar is soused."

& the Wackos weren't getting no commands from the Great Ash, so they put away their instruments and squished towards the door.

DADDY: (Legs spread to stop up doorway.) "YOU, not so fast."
DEVIL-SHIRT: "Hey man, move aside—it's a free world."
DADDY: "NegaTIVE. It ain't a free world on THIS property—it's $40 a night. This time when you people get out, you'll STAY out. Got it?"
WACKOS: (Rolling eyes.) "Like, GRUNT, GRUNT, GROAN, GROAN, man."
DADDY: I'll take that for a yes. (He steps aside, Wackos leave, he turns to Ash.) Now. YOU can get offen your lazy ass and clean up this mess, and you can—"

ASH: (Not moving, mouth hardly moving.) "YOU . . . can . . . BOW . . . to the . . . High Priest . . . of Egypt."

That done it for Deena. Boy, was she ugly. On top of High Priest Ash like you was a tomcat in the wrong neighborhood. Pounding to the rhythm of her screaming. "I HATE you, I HATE you, you RUINT our LIFE, you SONuvaBITCH, you RUINT our LIFE! WHY DON'T YOU JUST—" Well, I'll just say it got worse. Finally Mama & Daddy & me managed to pry Deena offen you and drag her upstair. She bawled in her room the rest of the night, didn't even come out to eat or call Kenneth.

You didn't move, not so much as a wince, just set like a statue while Deena went at you and afterwards while Mama cleaned the blood offen your face & put Bactine on the trenches Deena's fingernails dug out. You didn't say a word to let on you heard Mama say how worried we'd been all the time you was missing and how much more worried we was now that you come home in this condition.

We cleaned up around you. Then Daddy lugged you to the couch so he could take the keg back for the deposit $. Mama put out all the lights after supper so we wouldn't attract no Trick-or-Treaters—we'd had enough of freaks for one day. I slept in 9 cause I couldn't stand to hear Deena bawling no more. Also it'd be bad luck to leave Libby's entirely empty.

Me & Deena spent all the next day down at Grammy Ethyl's eating fudge.

February 13

Well, here goes. THAT night.

It was already getting pretty cold down cellar, and Daddy thought heating the basement all night was quite the frill when he spent good money keeping it perfectly warm upstair. I heaped quilt after quilt on, but the night after you was the High Priest of Egypt no amount of bedding could suck the chill out of my nose & toes. My rear was sweating, however, or maybe the couch was still soused to the gills. So I went up to my own bed, and when I got there I known without a doubt that you was really, seriously, completely

I don't know if I can write this part.

February 14

Happy Valentines
Violets are blue
And roses are red
When they ain't dead.

February 15

Last year we got this new health teacher, Mr. Sands. He was average height and average looking, but he was so quiet & puny, all the guys called him Mr. Sandface. Cause if he was in a cartoon, he'd be the 90-pound weakling getting sand kicked in his eyes. Lo & behold, this year

Mr. Sands come back to school Mr. Sandkicker. All muscles and strutting cocky. Movie-star handsome and seeming six foot tall. Girls started calling him a hunk. Everyone thought it was a bona fide miracle till Mr. Sands admitted he'd spent the summer at the gym lifting weights.

Well, I figured if puny Mr. Sandface could become a hunk over the summer, I could get rid of the roll around my gut and grow shoulders wider than my hips. Last week I started working out at the gym with Mr. Sands and a couple of other guys after the football players clear outa there. "Quiet-type time," Mr. Sands calls it. I'm glad I'm getting to know those guys. They're working hard, waiting for a great event to happen, and when it happens they're gonna be ready.

Today I was outa clean clothes so I had to break down and wear one of your old Knights of Sisyphus T-shirts to the gym.

"What's the Knights of SISSY-FUSS?" asked Mr. Sands. Which is exactly the sorta question why I never wanted to wear that shirt.

"Well, you know the Knights of Columbus?" Explaining it took me back to the days when you played with the Upcountry Boys, and the future was all hope. Sometimes I wish I could be stuck back then and live there forever. But that'd be numb, wouldn't it? I'd be stuck forever wishing I was grown up.

Anyways, Mr. Sands got such a kick out of your Knights of Sisyphus T-shirt that he wanted one. "That's the perfect weight lifters' shirt," he says. "We're alot like Sisyphus, except instead of pushing a rock uphill we push ourselves to put off old age and death. For awhile it might LOOK like we're getting somewhere, but in the end we all go downhill. Weight lifters exercise in futility."

You can tell Mr. Sands is a teacher, even when he's in the weight room.

I let him have the shirt.

A few minutes ago Mama walked in with an armload of sheets, without knocking, and seen me writing this. "What you doing, Wes?" she says.

I looked at her. "Sherlock Libby you ain't."

She come peeking over my shoulder, and I shoved the book into my desk drawer.

Mama put her hand on my cheek. "I'm sorry, Wes. I didn't mean to be minding your business. It's just . . ."

I know what IT'S JUST. She has to be careful now, watch for signs that I'm gonna be like you. Could happen. Wouldn't be fair, though, to get THAT but not perfect pitch and all A's. Mama feels guilty that she didn't see them signs the doctor said you was probably flashing when you was a teenager. Mostly she just feels guilty, especially since we seen this TV show say IT's always the PARENTS' fault.

Daddy says, "Bonnie, do you believe everything you see on unknown satellite TV? If this quackpot was any good he'd be on PBS, or at least on a network."

I says maybe you coulda been flashing signs all

through high school, but I never seen none before the day we hit the moose. And then it was too late.

February 16

It's suppose to snow all night—probably won't be no school tomorrow. I like snow. When I was little you use to take me snowmobiling winter nights after supper. You'd stuff me into one of them god-awful snowsuits that pinched under the arms, and I'd be on my knees in front of you. Musta been real comfortable with my boots jammed into your crotch.

I thought I was driving cause you let me press the throttles with your hands over mine. Even inside 3 pairs of mittens Grammy knit and Mama made me wear, my thumbs got so cold they hurt. When the hurt stopped, you says, "Dead thumbs—time to let Ash old boy drive." I'd put my hands on the engine then. I never felt more alive.

To this day whenever my thumbs get cold, I'm right back on the Arctic Cat with you, Ash.

February 17

I was right, no school today. I walked my toboggan up to the Bible Baby-sitters Club. Pastor Pudgy had this idea that on snow days parents should drop kids off at church on their way to work so they won't have to miss time or leave kids home alone with idle hands in the devil's workshop. The teenagers take care of the young ones. We don't get no $—our pay is the warm feeling in our heart & the eternal reward of taking the high road to the hereafter.

Personally, I like the excuse to play with the little shits all day—they know how to have fun. Unlike a certain benchwarmer I know.

On them Arctic Cat rides of yours and mine we'd end up at the snowmobile club for a hot chocolate and a couple hands of cribbage. I didn't play no cribbage, but it felt good to thaw out in a room with a real fire snapping & smelling of cedar. My word, it was fun watching you sort your cards, throw 2 into the kitty, peg your 31 for 2 and 1 for last card, count out your 15-2's & runs & pairs. They still talk about it up to the VF hall sometimes, how this little Libby kid whooped Suds Woodbrey. Best player in the club, Suds—he even won a tournament down to Portland. Do you still play cribbage, Ash, where you are?

February 18

Today the snow's 1/2 up the living room window—reminds me of that other time you saved my life. The winter me & Merle was 6. Well, that time it weren't literal about you saving my life—what you saved me from was Mama & Daddy KILLING me.

The wind offen the ocean always plows the snow right along the ridge we live on, and the back of the house stops a good pile of it. Once me & Merle climbed straight up a snowdrift and onto the roof. A roof knee-deep in snow ain't the best footing for a 1st grader wearing boots 1/2 a size too big so he can grow into them. I fell on my rear. The harder I tried to get up, the faster my snowsuit slid me downroof. Scared! I just known the landing would be the final act of Wesley William Libby, age 6. But it weren't. It was like landing waist-high in Marshmallow Fluff. So much fun, I couldn't wait to go at it again.

The only problem was, when I got out of my Marshmallow crater, my boots wasn't with me. Didn't take long for my stocking feet to get the weather report. But I couldn't go inside without them boots or I known I wouldn't be seeing nothing of Bugs Bunny & friends for awhile. Merle & me went bottoms up to paw around for the boots. No use—they was avalanched. By the time Mama come looking for us, tears was frozen in my hair and I couldn't tell whether my feet was still attached.

She run me inside and nursed the blood back into my toes while Daddy went digging for boots. But they stayed right where they was till the spring thaw. And I stayed right in my room till Mama & Daddy thawed. To keep my school shoes dry till the folks could afford new boots, I had to wear Wonder bread bags with rubber bands around the ankles.

"If I ever catch you sliding down that roof again I'll break your neck. If you haven't already broke it," says Mama. Handing me my replacement boots.

It's hard to resist a temptation that's right over your head night & day, especially when the folks are off at an Upcountry Boys gig and Grammy Ethyl who loves you & don't know the rules of the roof is watching you all afternoon. Only actually she's on the phone with Auntie Opal. Merle & me decided to risk it. Once. We just wouldn't land feet-1st and lose our boots.

"We'll go head-1st," I says.

"And lose our hat? No way," says Merle. "Butts-1st."

A butt ain't as easy to aim off a roof as you might think. We done pretty good, though. Enough to risk a 2nd slide. And a 3rd. And—you get the drift. Once & awhile my legs got stuck at the knees. In which case I'd hang on to one boot with both hands and pull out that foot real slow. Then repeat on the other side. We slid till dark and still had our boots on when we went in.

Well, you know how it is when you give in to temptation. If at 1st you don't get caught, you'll try, try again. The next time the folks left me & Merle home with a fresh snowdrift, you was watching us. Only you was actually playing guitar. Merle & me was wicked proud of ourself for getting away with sliding offen the roof yet another afternoon. Merle, he got a little cocky. Done a somersault & landed on his back.

"And you thought SLIDING off was fun," he says.

After that I couldn't just slide off and look like a pantywaist—I done a somersault too. And landed like a cat. On my feet. Them new replacement boots was in DEEP. I didn't even try to climb out, just stayed glued in the Marshmallow Fluff and bawled till you come to shovel me out.

"Wes, my man, you were sticking outa the snow like a bust of Beethoven on a white piano," you says that night in bed.

Bust of Little Wes Beethoven

You was serious, though, when you added that you better not catch me near that roof again, or else you'd have to tell Mama & Daddy, cause jumping offen a roof was a dumb thing to do, snow or no snow.

But that time you didn't tell. You saved my neck.

February 19

Okay, Wes old boy, just jump off into THAT night.

Everyone says I shouldn't feel bad—it was a good thing I found you when I did.

What I seen, the night after you was the High Priest of Egypt and my nose was froze but my rear was sweating so I went up to my own bed, was all the lights on and you huddled naked in the corner. You had a squiggle of cigarette ash on your thigh, and the scrid of the butt was still between your fingers. Your eyes was open, but they didn't look like there was nobody behind them.

I screamed.

Pretty soon Deena was screaming behind me.

"Good Lord, he's OD'd," says Mama. Pushing by me. She shook you, she yelled at you, but nobody would show up behind them eyes. Daddy unpinched your fingers. Red, blistered. Mama brushed the ashes offen your leg. Raw, oozy. Dark spots like the dirt in a hooked worm. We all winced. Except you.

Mama wrapped herself around you and rocked till the ambulance come.

February 20

I don't know what went on down to the state hospital. I weren't allowed to go. Mama rode with you in the ambulance, Daddy followed in the Blazer. But 1st Mama called Grammy Ethyl to come over and "keep Wes and Deena company." Keep us from breaking to pieces if Mama had to call home with worst news, more like.

I went to bed and got something like sleep. Nightmare, wake up. Nightmare, wake up. Might as well of spent the night trying to swim laps in ice—that's how cold & tired I felt in the morning. Finally fell into some dark sleep after Grammy Ethyl took pity and let us stay home from school. Mama & Daddy rolled in around noon. I hopped outa bed to find out what happened.

Mama's face was puffy, cheeks overfilling her skin like a microwaved hot dog. Daddy had the worst case of spider face I ever seen. Grammy took one look at him, says, "Steve dear, you been crying!" and run to hug him. Then Mama was a crying mess and we was all squeezed into a standing pig-pile. The smell of Mama's hair made me feel a little better, but not much. Me & Deena & Grammy was sure you was dead.

"Oh God," snuffed Deena, "I wish I never—"

Mama interrupted with a nose honk into a tissue. "Oh, honey, you got the wrong idea. Ash isn't dead. He didn't even OD. He's . . . he's hm—hm—hm . . ."—whimpering on the "m" like it was boiling soup. Her chin simmered on my shoulder. I known the word she was after. "Mental," I says.

Mama set down in a chair and nodded. "H-mentally ill."

Daddy pulled out of the hug pile and poured him & Mama some coffee. "Here we took him to get his stomach pumped, and no drugs was in his system at all. He weren't lying about being clean. They say he's got SCHIZOID TENDENCIES. Whatever them are."

At the time I didn't know what them words meant neither, except funny in the head. Now I know. Hearing things. Seeing things. Saying shocking things. Thinking you're someone you ain't. Thinking people are talking about you when they ain't. Hyped up or zombied down. You, after the moose.

"Well now, Ashton's always been awful intelligent & high-strung," says Grammy Ethyl. "He's DIFFERENT, but that ain't mental illness. When Mama had a mere nervous breakdown they put her in BMHI," (this was the aforementioned time I got Great-Grammy Avis's address) "and they didn't let her out till her own funeral. You better be care—"

"Mother! Please! This ain't Grammy Avis." Daddy leaned his forehead against the wall. Tapping. Almost bashing. "We shoulda trusted Ash wouldn't choose to be on drugs. He took them cause this schizoid thing chose HIM. It's a disease! I shouldn't of hauled him inside on Wes's birthday, I shoulda hauled him to the hospital."

"Now Daddy," says Deena. "It ain't your fault nobody seen what ailed him. This ain't the chicken pox."

Mama put her hand on Daddy's arm. "In case you didn't know, Steve Libby, sometimes that smart mouth of hers isn't stupid."

February 21

We thought you was ruining yourself with drugs before, and now drugs was fixing you. The drugs they put you on to get you moving got you moving 3 days after you got to the hospital. The 1st thing you says was, "Wes, where's my guitar?" The 2nd thing was, "I want my schoolbooks."

The books was a go. But they didn't let nobody on the psychiatric ward have nothing so dangerous as guitar strings. Took away somebody's ceramic music box cause a patient had broke the little ballerina offen one and stuck the jagged edge into her neck. No shampoo or aftershave in glass bottles, neither—everything had to be plastic. Daddy give you the (cordless) electric razor to use, and every morning he come to breakfast with bloody toilet paper dots on his chin. For once I was glad to have a baby's-bottom face.

"If they don't want him knocking hisself off, I don't see why they let him smoke a carton of cigarettes a day," says Deena.

No smoking allowed anywheres except the TV lounge, but everyone carried so much smoke around in their hair & clothes that the entire ward smelt like an ashtray anyways. Yours was the only ward in the hospital that allowed ANY smoking. Guess they didn't dare to let you outside where they made the normal smokers hide.

I take it back—there was one non-chain-smoker on the ward, your roommate, what's-his-name. That short skinny guy with the big eyes? He wandered around shouting, "This is hell! Look at the sulfur coming from those devils' mouths! Look, I'm in hell!"

A few days after you come to, you got on the doctors to let you out so you wouldn't have to quit college. They admired your Yankee ingenuity. Besides, Thanksgiving was coming. They sent you home with some prescriptions and appointments for counseling.

My word, we had hope then. Hope that you'd get better now that they was treating what really ailed you. In Mama's latest library research we read that schizoid patients broke into 3rds: 1/3 get better, 1/3 never get better, 1/3 go off & on. We hoped you was in the 1st 3rd, and why not, you was always at the top of everything else you done. We hoped you'd come home good old Ash old boy and we'd pick up Libby life where it left off before you hit the moose. We had all this hope even though they didn't take care of it at the hospital.

No guitar cause someone could hang themself on the strings? Your roommate, maybe, to get out of hell. Not my brother. Not Ash.

Amazing, the Ash that come home less than 2 weeks after being hauled away looking comatose. Them must of
been some drugs cause they OVERcured you. "PET
scanning has determined that schizophrenics do not me-
tabolize glucose equally in all parts of the brain & that
drug treatment can bring improvement to those regions,"
says Deena.

You was wicked energetic, never tired. Always moving. Not like the beginning of the summer, though. You
was back to 3 baths a day, but quick ones. Run the tub,
splash around, and out. Always home before 11 and never
with party stench or bloodshot eyes. Too bad Krista had
already give up—she mighta liked you this way. You even
helped make Thanksgiving dinner.

All my life Grammy Ethyl's ample side of the family
has come to Libby's for Thanksgiving vacation days.
They fill the house, they fill most of the units (ain't many
paying customers then), they'd probably fill the sites too
if it wasn't too cold & dangerous to camp out during
hunting season. Grammy Ethyl's side of the family's so
filling, it's the only time of year we all get together, unless there's a funeral or wedding or coincidence.

Remember when we all run into each other at Fen-
way Park? Daddy just had to watch the Red Sox beat
the Yankees, and you & me wasn't gonna miss that, and
Mama & Grammy wasn't gonna miss a stop at Faneuil

"Fan-Your-Money" Hall. Deena didn't even mind staying home to tend desk for some reason, har-de-har-har. (This was right before she brung The Hormone home to misstate his intentions.) Anyways, turns out every single family in the family had seats up behind 1st base. "Ain't it a small world!" Auntie Opal kept saying to Auntie Audrey. "Too small," you whispered to me.

When you come home from the hospital acting energetic, we had plenty to be thankful for without Thanksgiving on top of it. I overheard the folks talking it over. They was a little worried about how you might act.

We all hoped you was back to your old self, but we didn't have amnesia about the guy who showed up in your birthday suit at my party, neither.

Daddy called up his sisters & brothers & aunts & uncles & cousins to tell them we decided to have Thanksgiving alone this year. He weren't off the phone 1/2 an hour before Grammy Ethyl rammed in, all bent out of shape. "Well look now, Bonnie," she says, "I can see why you wouldn't want to do all that cooking after all you been through, but the rest of us will pitch in. Thanksgiving's the only time I ever get to see my whole family together. I already bought my film! The trailer ain't big enough for everyone to set down and eat in, but I can do the turkey in my oven, and . . ."

Meanwhile, Mama was sliding this confused look between Daddy & Grammy Ethyl, trying to figure out how Bonnie Libby got to be the Grinch Who Stole Thanksgiving. Daddy shrugged every time the look swung his way. Grammy didn't even notice it, just kept narrating.

Daddy cleared his throat and put his hand on Grammy's shoulder. "Mother, it's not the money and not that Bonnie don't wanna cook. We—I—don't want a crowd in the house till Ash is squared away. You seen how he, well, you know. Acts. Sometimes."

"You mean to tell me the family has to go 2 years without getting together cause Ash ain't got aholt of his-self yet? You're the man of the house—you just tell him to straighten hisself out so we can have a nice Thanksgiv-ing." She leaned ahead & lowered her voice like she was passing on a secret she shouldn't be. "You know, some-times kids will do ANYTHING to get attention."

Major Mama stared THE LOOK at Daddy. Her lips curled into French position. But he didn't seem able to move HIS lips. Like the time General Grammy lit into him for letting Deena go out with a Pike, "cause you know what the father was like—don't let the mother fool you."

"I can't believe you said that, Ethyl," says Mama. "No offense, but you obviously have no idea what Ash's problem is."

"We got some informative reading material right here, if you—" started Deena, but Grammy was already full steam ahead.

"What Ash's whole problem is, is you're too soft on him, that's what. It's none of my business, and I've never interfered, but I always thought you spoilt them kids. You let them—"

Suddenly Mama opened the door and crooked her finger at me. "Sorry to cut you off, Ethyl, but there's somewhere I gotta be with Wes." THE FINAL LOOK at Daddy, and then I found out where Mama walks off her mad spells. Speed-walked up to Cavalry without saying a word—I couldn't hardly keep up with her.

Mama got the key from under the bottled gas cover out back. Inside she set staring out the coat-of-many-colors window. Sun stains on her face. So pretty.

I picked out "The Old Rugged Cross" on the piano and thought about what you'd say. "You'd have perfect pitch this time, Wes old boy, if you'd hit the right notes."

Finally Mama said she'd figured out what to have for protein tomorrow—baked beans—and we'd better get back to sort & soak them.

Grammy was gone. "I don't think we'll be seeing much of my mother for awhile," says Daddy. "She'll be punishing me by staying away. I didn't follow orders."

"It's about time," says Mama.

February 23

The day before Thanksgiving Grammy insisted on coming over to help clean the 2 units that had customers. Pretending she hadn't spent the week pretending we didn't exist. Deena was trying to watch a soap-scum opera, and I was laying on the sitting couch with my toes jammed between her ribs like you taught me, when who rolls in the driveway but carloads of Daddy's sisters &

brothers & nieces & nephews & aunts & uncles & cousins.

Me & Deena curled up our lip at each other and run to warn Mama.

"I don't get it," she says, looking out the door of 6. Smiling and waving to Uncle Jo-Jo & Auntie Audrey & all their little thumb-suckers.

"I told everyone to come up anyways and check into Libby's as paying customers, since the owners didn't invite them," says Grammy, scrubbing a hole through 6's tub. I think she didn't want to look Mama in the eye. Mama wanted to look her in the eye, though. Leaned all the way to the soap dish.

"You didn't," says Mama.

"You folks can still have your Thanksgiving alone together, and the rest of us will go out to Helen's Famous Restaurant," Grammy was saying. "Don't know why I never thought of that before. So much easier!" Tossed me her Comet-blue rag and a-hugging she went.

"She did," I says.

For just a second, Mama went slack like she was leaking air. Then she filled back out and says, "I'll have to take care of her later. Wes, come help me do some grocery shopping. Deena, go help everyone settle into rooms, and don't let them give you a penny or a credit card. As long as they're already here, we might as well have Thanksgiving-as-usual."

The next 96 hours, me, Deena & the folks was just waiting for the 2nd coming of Jesus Ash. Or the emperor in his no clothes. Or the High Priest of Egypt in a trance. Or some worse shock we couldn't even imagine yet.

What you done was roll pie pastry and hack apart rock-hard squash and baste turkey when all the other men was out trying to shoot deer. Nobody ever gets nothing, but that's the Thanksgiving ritual. Men hunt. Women cook. Children peel vegetables in front of the TV parades or go outside and try to play hide & seek in bright orange coats. (What they're really hiding from is potatoes, carrots & especially turnips.)

I coulda gone hunting that year—I was old enough—but after the Blazer incident I didn't like the idea. I peeled.

"Ash, why ain't you out hunting with the rest of the boys?" says Daddy's O-bese sister Opal in her Oh-how-Auntie-loves-you voice.

One of your smiles CREEPED up on her. "The eyes of God are in the face of every living creature, Aunt Opal. God's eyes aren't bull's-eyes."

The Aunties & Grammy hee-honked like you was the old Ash talking, the one popping jokes all over. Me, Deena & Mama didn't laugh. We known you meant it.

"You got a point," says Auntie Opal. "Good thing the butcher cut the head offen that turkey, or you'd be basting God's eyes right this minute," and the laughter pealed.

You still had your smile on but didn't say nothing out loud, just whispered to me, "They don't understand that the Thanksgiving turkey is a sacrifice, not an execution. Its life is given up like prayer."

Except for little things like that, and Grammy's wet eyes when she come back from a little walk with Mama, it was Thanksgiving-as-usual.

February 24

That Sunday the carloads of family headed south for the winter, and you headed off for your 1st Sunday of church hopping. Your plan was to fan out to every church in Maine by day and fan back into home by night. Like so:

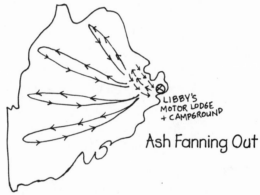

Ash Fanning Out

It weren't that you had to keep looking to find God, neither, cause you seen God everywheres. But there was a big problem.

"Every church twists off a piece of God and worships it," you told me. "It's gonna take the rest of my life, but I'm going to every church in every religion in the world to collect the pieces, and when I'm done I'll put God back together so people will understand the whole of creation."

I was thinking God oughta go around and collect your pieces and put YOU back together, but I just smiled and waved you off.

February 25

Meanwhile, back in Calvin Cove Thanksgiving Sunday, Pastor got another 20 minutes' worth laid on him in the vestibule while he was shaking hands with the incomers. "A godsend for them that like their pot roast rare," he says. "The young's our future," announced like he'd discovered some truth nobody ever told us before, "and I have to tell you, folks, God is very VERY VERY troubled about the young people in the Cavalry family."

Deena squirmed into me squirming into her.

There was only 2 pews that didn't jiggle by the time he was done, the ones full of the busload from Sweet Acres Retirement Home who had nothing to worry about.

The Lord had revealed to Pastor that some certain young people of the congregation was taking wrong paths on their pilgrimage to the afterlife, which was only natural in this corrupt world of ours where Satan was bulldozing false paths all over and paving them to look like the highway to heaven. The devil's been working 24 hours a day to make the map to heaven real hard to read. Cigarette and beer companies trying to recruit kids in commercials with cartoons, children's books with swear words and no Christian lesson, schools sending young people to hell with prophylactic demonstrations instead of making a case for the Lord's blessed matrimonial bed.

"It's all the devil's work," he says. "And there's only one way to stop Satan's powerful tentacles from splitting the personalities and the very souls of our young people. Their fathers MUST get right with the Lord cause it's God's word that the father is the head of the family, and the sins of the father are visited on the sons. And daughters."

There was a lot of page turning and quoting along in here. But for once Mama weren't taking notes. Her fingers was white fists in the crotch of her Bible.

"Don't take it personal," I whispered. "He's probably talking about Shawn Fox."

Mama smiled at me, but she shouldn't of cause after church we found out the pastor meant her to take it personal. On the way out he asked would Mama & her other 1/2 have some free time after the roast for a visit. Mama made an EEK face and says, "Good Lord! After THAT sermon? Bradley Lovell, you know how he feels about your witnessing."

There was water in his eyes, put the fire right out. "Please, Bonnie. This ain't your minister talking—it's Steve's old friend."

Mama bit her lips as she stared into his begging eyes. Then she nodded once and turned away quick. I couldn't see her face.

In the parking lot we got a GRASP of whose hand-shaking had laid the 20 minutes on Pastor Pudgy. Mrs. Fish-Lips snatched aholt of Mama's elbow and says, "Land a Goshen, I'm awful sorry to hear Ash has a split personality." Face all wrinkled in pity like you had AIDS.

Split personality! Split from reality, you was. Dr. Jekyll &/or Mr. Hyde, you wasn't. If I had Deena's mouth, I'd of spouted off an "In-case-you-didn't-know, Mrs. Pike, _____ ain't _____." Still ain't thought of nothing good to fill in the blanks.

"I'm awful sorry to hear you heard that, Mrs. Pike," says Mama, "since it ISN'T true." Mama always says "isn't," but I think "ain't" sounds better. More natural.

Mrs. Pike's scaly eyebrows practically hit her wig. "Oh?"

"Generally I find it sickening to gossip about any-one's medical problems, but I'll make an exception this once to let you know that a split personality isn't one of Ash's," says Mama. "It's a real shame people don't spread their rumors straight."

"Ash DOES have schizophrenia, don't he?" Mrs. Pike looking fishy at Kenneth when she says this.

Meanwhile, Mama was giving THE LOOK to Deena. We wasn't suppose to tell people nothing specific about what you had. It was none of their damn business and besides, if you give people a label, they'll stick it to you. Jane Murphy's in the National Honor Society, but the clique idiots still call her "retard" behind her back cause she stayed behind in Ist & 2nd grade. Thank God I never had to stay back. Closest I ever come to the honor roll is reading it in the hallway.

I don't know what Pastor Pudgy told Mama & Daddy when he come over that afternoon. They sent me out to dust flushes (most of them wasn't used for weeks). But he musta found that soft spot with his name on it in Daddy's heart, cause the Sunday after Mrs. Fish-Lips had the INFINITESIMAL GILLS to tell the pastor you had a split personality, Daddy went to church. And Christmas weren't for another 3 weeks.

February 26

Daddy's an all-or-nothing sorta guy. From church twice a year to twice every Sunday and once on Wednesday. I started calling him Fish Food cause of Mrs. Pike's new refrain, "Why Steve Libby, it's food for my soul seeing you here AGAIN this WEEK!"

His idea of saying grace use to be, "God helps them who help themself. So help yourself." Now when he blesses the food, I pray that it don't get cold.

Deena says this ABOUT-FACE is only natural, given his military training.

Yesterday I watched this Warner Brothers cartoon where Daffy Duck & Porky Pig are prisoner in a sky-scraper. No matter what they do to escape, the evil building manager is there blowing cigar smoke in their face and hooking them back up to leg chains. Finally they call up Bugs Bunny for advice cause HE can squeeze out of anything. At lst you don't see Bugs, just hear his voice coming out of the phone.

He asks if they tried the elevator. Of course good ole Daffy and Porky tried that. Did they try shoving the bully down the stairs? Yup, tried that. And how about swinging across to the next building on a rope? Yup again.

"Dey didn't work, did dey."

Then you see Bugs is in the next room hooked up to a leg chain too. Depressing! Reminded me of Togo after he chewed through his rope. The chain or the box? Guess there ain't that much difference between a hero & a dog. SUPERMAN bit the big one. Even Jesus couldn't chew loose of his nails.

While I was watching cartoons Daddy was copying a form letter out in his own penmanship. Begging Grammy Ethyl to get truly saved so she'll be one of the Whosoevers there to greet us at the pearly gates. The religious magazine Daddy found it in says the letter's over 50% effective in softening hard hearts to Christ and turning strong wills into fertile ground like a child's soul. I can see why—lines like, "We will all live forever spiritually, (name of loved one). I want my whole family to live with God." But I don't think Grammy Ethyl will appreciate the letter, she ain't exactly planning on heading south for eternity.

Daddy's worried cause she ain't gone down to the

front of the church since she was a kid. Even though she wears cross earrings and sends 70¢/day to the Christian Children's Fund so a starving child will learn to read the Bible. This is one area where Grammy Ethyl prides herself on tight lips cause, "Religion is personal private, and nobody can know the state of nobody else's soul." But Pastor says this ain't the way of a TRUE Christian. A TRUE Christian can't help but witness and proclaim to the world and attend Sunday & Wednesday fellowship regular, cause the Holy Spirit puts the car keys in their hands and MOVES them right into the car and along the highway to heaven.

Jesus does save people, though. From hell on earth if not the underworld. Cause if you truly believe in his power, you got peace of mind no matter what shit happens. I think Daddy needed the peace so bad he HAD to believe, or lose hope. Hopeless ain't no way to live. Worse'n a dog on a chain.

February 27

Even if he ain't rocking & rolling with Wackos, and streaking, and speaking unmentionables, a schizoid-tended guy who's gonna put God together like Humpty-Dumpty ain't exactly in the top 3rd. You was better to live with, but you wasn't BETTER.

How can I describe the constant motion you was in? Not just frantic fanning out to churches in all your spare time. When you was folded in to home, you hardly slept. Day & night you was always muttering things like "It's in the Phoenix's wings" or "burdocks" or "around the circle twice." The Ash breeze was just a-whipping.

You, me & Mama was slavering jam on hot-buttered English muffins for the breakfast baskets one morning, and out of nowheres you says, "We are all raspberry seeds doing our own thing. Isolated. Alone. While the fruit evolves for God's digestion."

"Really," says Mama. "That's interesting."

Sounded suspiciously like one of them poems Miss Small's always trying to convince us we should get alot outa. Sure, I can figure out the words by themself.

WE = me plus some yous.

SEEDS = things that get around and grow into FRUITS just like their parents.

EVOLVES = survival of the fittest, natural selection, improvement of the species, etc. Even though Pastor corrected that for us in Sunday School, "Genesis is the best science & history book ever written. Fossils and dinosaur bones were planted by the devil to snare geniuses into hell."

DIGESTION = what happens to grub between the kitchen and the toilet.

But string them all together and forget it. Me & all the yous are all planted here to change into God food? I don't get it.

February 28

Today is the almost-anniversary of a day I'll never forget. But I'm gonna give it a try anyways.

March 1

In December Miss Small made us write a poem about words. I didn't know nothing about words so I got a library book to INSPIRE me, meaning "to blow or breathe an idea into one's head." The book said a related word meant "to break wind." Which explains the grade I got.

The Words of God
by Wes Libby
Words are born & grow & change,
Sometimes they even die of old age.
They also have a family tree.
So you can trace their history.

The <u>write</u> word use to mean to scratch,
Old English men use to do just that.
And then they'd <u>erasus</u>, (scratch out, in Latin),
Cause they was writing on tablets waxen.

And <u>comma</u> meant a piece cut off,
I cut off alot of pieces I shouldn't of.

Here are some histories of words religious.
Which Pastor would probly make me erasus.
(To me the Bible's like the Tower of Babel.
A place where words ain't quite understandable.)

Old English bledsian *means to consecrate*
 in blood,
"God bless our troops!" says, "God bathe them
 in blood!"
People praying don't know what they're saying,
Everytime they "bless the food."

Inspiratio *means under the influence,*
Of divine ideas breathed in by a god.
And if you are inspired you are a prophet.
(Unless you're faking and in it for profit.)

P.S. *means post script, or writ in after,*
Here is something I thought of later.
The capital G makes god more important.
Which I noticed too about Winnie-the-Pooh.

Miss Small writ: F

Because of references to your personal situation, to
say nothing of your distinctive style of grammar and
mechanics, it is evident that you tried and failed to
make someone else's words your own. The rhymes,
rhythms and ideas are much more sophisticated than

you have demonstrated yourself capable of in past work. Perhaps you got a bit too much help from Ash? I do like this poem, Wesley; however, I simply cannot permit you to get away with literary theft. Plagiarism is unacceptable. You may hand in another original work in its place if you wish.

I didn't wish, and I told her so. Also, I done that poem all by myself and never even SHOWN it to you (till now, which may be never). I even lent her the library book that INSPIRED it, and she still didn't believe me. But she caved in & give me my usual C minus anyways cause she didn't have a copy of whatever I supposedly copied, and she couldn't prove All-A's Ash helped me, neither.

Why's my life gotta be all tied up with yours like that? Course Miss Small was right in a way she didn't mean—I couldn't of writ that poem without you being funny in the head. Which got me to THINKING.

PARADOX: If Miss Small wanted to catch a cheater, she shoulda looked in MY Bible and seen the poem about words MERLE handed in. I didn't tell her the 2 of us writ it together the last Sunday I was 13.

Roast in Heaven
*There once was a Pastor from Maine
Who said it again and again:
"If you live by God's word
Then let it be heard,
There's a roast waiting for you in heaven!"*

You just can't Judas on your best friend, even if you ain't his no more. Even if it's eating away at your stomach till the ache moves up into your head. Mama kept asking me why I was losing weight. "So Deena can find it," I says. Mama had enough aches & pains of her own without mine on her mind.

March 2

Mr. Zippy Ash got all A's on final exams, which averaged out good with all the F's Mr. Zombie Ash had got during the semester. Too bad YOU couldn't average out like your grades.

The l0th of December your semester was done and you didn't have noplace you had to be for awhile (except for the pharmacy and the counselor's office, which I'll get back to later). Everyday you took off church hopping. The lst couple nights you did come home. Then you says, "I'd better keep fanning out instead of folding in."

You packed up your guitar and a duffel bag and off you went in your rusty blue Nova. We never seen that car again. But I'm aheada myself.

All we heard from you till Christmas was picture postcards that took so long getting to our mailbox that Mama said the employees in all the PO's between the postmark and Calvin Cove musta been taking them home to show their friends. They was actual Kodak pictures, each one the back of a car that had a minimum of one bumper sticker &/or custom license plate. These items stuck to a certain theme.

A little sardine can of a car with more stickers than chrome, in case anyone missed the message:

God answers prayers—
JUST ASK HIM!

Jesus is just
a prayer away....

Home is where
the Lord is.

I'm the flesh &
blood of Christ.

When it's all over,
where will YOU be?

KIDS NEED
TO PRAY

Families that stay together
pray together.

FAITH or FEAR?
It's your choice.

A Mack truck that looked like this:

 START YOUR WEEK OFF RIGHT
ATTEND THE CHURCH OF YOUR CHOICE

A BMW with too much taste to plaster a sticker on their bumper—they had a special license plate:

SAVED

A Cadillac lemon that coulda been Noah's Ark—the woman standing next to it looked like she belonged on the boat beside the other St. Bernard:

Don't be caught dead
without JESUS!

On the backs of these photos you just writ our address and one sentence of Humpty-Dumpty. Daddy took to throwing them in the trash after the one of a Ford pickup with a gun rack across the back window:

I'm in the
LORD'S army.

SUPPORT AMERICA'S FINEST

Daddy thrown that card out cause what you writ on the back was, "These people think that they are the only sheep, but J.C. himself said (if we can trust John's word for it), 'And other sheep I have, which are not of this fold [note: fold means religion or continent or raspberry patch]: them also I must bring, and they shall hear my voice; and there shall be one fold, and one shepherd,' which hasn't happened yet so why don't Christians put away their damn guns & leave it to Jesus?"

Soon's Mama read that out at the supper table, Daddy told us to kneel, join hands and pray for your blasphemous & unpatriotic soul. "Lord," he shouted up to the ceiling fan, "if this is your way of telling me I ain't quite right with you yet, please hear my prayer: Have mercy on my family, who you are punishing for my sins. Show me how to set our house in order. Amen."

"Amen, but if you want my opinion," says Deena, as if anyone ever does, "the father being right or wrong with the Lord ain't got diddly-squat to do with raspberries in a kid's head."

We kept praying for a miracle anyways, everytime we got one of your bumper cards.

I dug them out of the trash and hid them out to the Shibboleth. So MERLE DAIGLE, if you're still reading this, which you know why you better not be, don't you dare go look for them.

The one week of the year Mama forgets customers exist is Christmas to New Year's. That's for family, she says, so we put a CLOSED sign on Libby's and head up to Caribou for a few days with Grammy & Grampy "Mountain Dew" Tibbetts. Grammy Ethyl complains, but not much, cause she's got Thanksgiving—she just waits her tree till we get back. But that year we didn't go up for Christmas cause Mama was too scared to leave the phone. Expected it to ring any minute with bad-Ash-news.

What little we was hearing FROM you was bad enough—what we heard ABOUT you was worse.

Your psychiatrist's secretary kept calling to ask why you wasn't at your appointments.

Mama called the pharmacist to check if you'd been refilling the prescriptions of them drugs that kept you moving. No, and there hadn't been no requests from other pharmacies to forward the prescriptions, neither.

We was worried that you'd just slow down and stop again, only we wouldn't be there to find you. Maybe nobody would. Daddy called the police to look for you. They said sorry, but even if he was schizoid tended, an 18-year-old taking off on his own weren't none of their business.

Christmas Eve was a real family-fun time. Grammy Ethyl never happier, narrating and picture-taking. "Now Deena, I want one of you in front of the Christmas tree, ain't got one of them since you was—a little to the left, dear. Course I'd never be a mother-in-law and intrude on the other side of my son's family, or—why ain't you showing them pretty Libby dimples now, Deena? ISN'T this the nicest Christmas we ever had, Steve? The real meaning of love and family comes through when times are bad and there ain't many presents under the tree. . . ."

Daddy & Mama just set behind their teeth, trying to look as happy as they oughta be on Christmas, even if their beloved son hadn't showed up yet or called to say he weren't coming.

But 5 A.M. Christmas you did call, collect, and sung your own rendition of "I Wish You a Merry Christmas" in a high-pitched voice that didn't belong to you. Maniac laughter at the end of each line. That's all Mama told me about the call. Whatever else you said, it weren't good for Mama's fingernails.

When I got REALLY worried was when your picture bumper cards started coming from New Hampshire post offices. One was an RV with a "You've Got a Friend in Pennsylvania" plate but "Pennsylvania" 1/2 covered over by one of them Christmas-tree-light license plate holders:

Must be a waiting list for that plate.

Now, I ain't counted, but if every town in Maine has as many churches as the towns around Calvin Cove, it shoulda took more than a few weeks for your fan to open out all the way to the state line. So when the news reporter called in the 1st week of January, it weren't exactly a shock to find out you wasn't still fanning out to find the pieces twisted offen God. The shock was finding out what you WAS doing in New Hampshire.

When the phone rung Mama was out delivering pies and Daddy was working 2nd shift at the cannery. It was prime Hormone time. Deena jumped on the phone, "Hello," all breath, hardly any voice box.

"No"—suddenly all voice box—"they ain't here." Pause, and Deena was using a CBS Evening News anchorwoman voice: "Could you please give me a moment to discuss this with my other brother?"

She smothered the talk piece in her ample bazoombas.

"A reporter for The New York Times wants to know how the family feels about that pain in the ASH running for PRESIDENT!?"

"Of what?" I says.

"Nothing embarrASHes him no more," she says to me. Then into the phone, "No comment."

Next day me & Daddy stopped at every store from here to Machias looking for The New York Times. Finally found it in the University of Maine library. Went there and skimmed every page every day for a week but didn't find nothing in there about you. Which made sense, since the cover of the newspaper said, "All the news that's fit to print."

Then one afternoon Grammy Ethyl come in with this newspaper a friend in NH sent her. <u>The New Age Times.</u> And on the cover a big picture of you with your prophet-face shining. Headline: "God Speaks Through Maine Youth."

The article went on for pages with stuff like the following. (I might not got it word for word—Grammy Ethyl done something with the original so Daddy wouldn't never find it and have a stroke.)

Q: Why are you campaigning in the presidential primaries even though you're barely 1/2 old enough?

A: God told me I have to lead the nation of nations in the task of putting God's pieces together.

Q: Ain't that more like a minister's job? What about the separation of church and state?

A: Look, all of humanity, not just one church in one religion, must evolve into a higher form! Our holy quest is to gather all the pieces of God which humans have scattered about the earth like so many burdocks and raspberry seeds. The president of the U.S. is the only single person with enough power to gather the pieces and spread the New Word.

Q: How do YOU know?

A: God is revealed direct to all people in their own time and place, and holy books such as the Bible are just a trace of that truth, laced with human opinion and hearsay. God is never silent to those of good faith who seek truth. . . .

The article went on so long, Deena & me wore out

our voice reading it aloud. You sounded like a real prophet, Ash, so real that it made me wonder if some of them guys who writ the Bible was schizoid tended too.

Pastor often says the Bible guys was "taking dictation from God." I ain't too smart, so I might be missing something, but if that's how God chose to get across the all-time truth, then he ain't got much common sense. Why didn't he dictate in English & French & Chinese and all the other languages that ever was or will be? No doubt about it, them'd be God's words, right in the preordained form, no questions asked. Why didn't he wait for them to invent TV and then send Jesus so the reporters would follow him around and show the miracles forever on reruns? At the very least he coulda made his son write everything down in his own words instead of blowing the idea into some other guys' heads long after Jesus was rose and gone.

God talks to you, you're nuts. God talks to Pastor Pudgy, he's ordained. Maybe what people THINK God laid on them ain't necessarily FROM God, just plain human inspiration like we all get. Or maybe it's ALL from God.

I known your presidential platform had some warped planks, Ash, don't get me wrong. But it also made some sense. Cause there's times I just know something better & stronger than me is out there, and what I know don't come from no holy books or no sermons. It comes from my BONES.

In January a UPS trucker dropped off a microwave oven box addressed to me. Inside, a little note from you— "Wes, need you to translate this for me"—on top of reams and reams of music paper covered with frantic squiggles. Even your handwriting had schizoid tendencies. Here's one I figured out:

I before E, except.
Turn the other cheek, except.

I thought maybe if I could play some of the music, the feelings would make sense to me. Like the day your soul was floating around on the dust in our room. I took my violin & some of the pages into the bathroom.

Sounded like a bunch of scraped-out notes. No melody at all. Probably I played off-key.

Went up to church to try your message out on the piano with perfect pitch. Still no soul. Probably hit the wrong notes.

Then I got it—you was writing in secret code. I checked a code-decoding book out of the library and spent hours trying to figure out nothing.

But it all meant something to you, I known. Was that God's pieces in the box? Too bad God don't speak English. Was that your testament I couldn't translate? I wished I could. I'd of believed you. But it's too late now—the box disappeared after Daddy was in our room fixing the radiator.

March 5

You didn't even come home for the beginning of your spring semester at college. In February, when you did manage to "drag ASH home" (says guess who), we could see they wouldn't have much use for you over to the university, anyways. Your batteries was dead.

Mama stepped out to get the newspaper and found you on the steps. Stiff like a Little Match Boy. In a bundle of rags. Hands froze around the neck of your guitar case. Staring off towards the Atlantic, like you was straining to see it beyond the hills & trees.

Who knows where your Nova was. Off in the burdocks and around the circle twice. So was you. We never even found out how you got home. "Jesus brung him home on the wings of our prayers," says Daddy.

Incidentally it was around in here that Jesus quit smoking. Okay, it was Daddy who quit—me & Deena just say it was Jesus. Daddy smoked for 30 years, then stopped cold turkey the day he put the addiction in the Lord's hands. After that he put on 20 pounds which he's now praying off. "Oh, how I love Jesus," Daddy sings. "Cause he sure took the pressure offen me."

"When Jesus comes again, his name should be WILL POWER," says Deena.

What I wanted to know is, if Jesus brung you home on wings of prayers then why didn't he fly you home CURED?

This time we didn't bother to call the ambulance to rush you to the emergency room. The folks loaded you into the Blazer and hauled you back to the smoke ward for some waking up.

The hospital took X rays and run loads of tests to make sure you wasn't actually paralyzed. You might as well of been. Took a week to get you to budge, and that day you moved just once, reaching up to shake my hand, with the slow tremble of a weight lifter benching too heavy.

The following days you'd talk a few minutes then lay on your bed, exhausted, for hours. Like you was making up for all them superhuman nights of staying up storming your brain, burning energy you shouldn't of had.

Never asked for your guitar. Maybe you just known it wouldn't be no use. No suicide strings allowed. But it still made me real sad to think you didn't ask.

March 6

The maniac laughter Mama had told us about Christmas Day was the first recognizable part of you to come back. You'd say things like, "I'm scared, hahaha!" Or, "Somebody please help me, hahaha!" "Bring me your breadbox to drown the voices, Wes, hahaha!" Sound effects for your creepy smile. And this state of mind was rubbing off on the whole family.

Mama was crying 1/2 the time and always on antibiotics for something-itis. Sinusitis, tonsillitis, otitis.

Deena weren't talking much, which was a blessing, but her mouth was still busy. She finished off my plate at every meal—I didn't have the stomach for it. Poor Deena was developing SUBSTANTIAL underpinnings. When Daddy weren't around, which was alot after he got hisself elected church deacon, Grammy Ethyl asked Deena if she might be eating for 2 and needing some woman-to-woman advice. Deena says, "For your information, Grammy, eating don't make you PREGNANT."

Now that you was so talkative, the King of the Smoke Ward decided it was time to get to the bottom of things with some "family counseling." King meaning the psychoanalyst named Dr. Finklestein—me & Deena took to calling him Frankenstein. He was too old to look anything like the mad doctor in the movie, but he did make monsters out of people.

The 5 of us Libbys would go into his office and sit in a circle while he asked questions. Some of his words rode on top of <u>underlines.</u>

Q1: Can anybody recall instances in Ashton's childhood when he was <u>overprotected,</u> not allowed to make his own choices?

Q2: Was Ashton ever physically <u>abused</u> or punished severely enough for him to feel <u>victimized?</u>

Q3: Were Mr. and Mrs. Libby ever so busy with work or with other children that they neglected Ashton's emotional needs?

The lst day, nobody could think of answers to these questions, except no. Dr. Franky said we was probably in denial or repressing these bad memories and to think about the Q's for next time.

The 2nd day, Deena put her 2¢ worth in on Q3. "Daddy & Mama was so busy getting Libby's going when we was little, we never went nowheres except school and church. Everyone else in 7th grade got to go roller skating Saturday nights."

Her ribs slipped into my elbow. This so-called family counseling weren't about her not being allowed at smoker-skating parties. Before Frankenstein could accuse the folks of child neglect, I says, "That ain't true— we went up to Caribou and down to Massachusetts to see relatives and the Red Sox all the time, and you know it. How else you think you got addicted to Fan-Your-Money Hall?"

The 3rd day, people on the ward were walking around with a black spot on their forehead. "ASH Wednesday—maybe this will be your lucky day," Deena told you. But it weren't.

Mama answered Ql. Like it was an essay question. "Well, I guess there were a few times you might say I overprotected him. When he was 5 Ash begged to go skiing with one of his kindergarten friends, and I didn't let him cause I was afraid he'd break his leg. He always begged

155

for Froot Loops and Cocoa Krispies, but I said no, they'll rot your teeth and ruin your taste buds for oatmeal. No band gigs without us to chaperone till he was 16, and things like that. All for his own good. I thought."

Dr. Franky tapped his pencil on his yellow pad and took a noisy breath through his nose. Pause. "Is that how you remember it, Ashton?"

You shrugged and let loose one of your maniac laughs.

"You see," says Dr. Franky to Mama, "you're what's called a <u>Domineering Mother.</u> Ashton hears a good many voices, but yours is the one that <u>restricts</u> him and tells him he <u>cannot</u> do things."

Mama dug up other instances of how she domineered you, such as no cowboy hat in church, no car keys of your own after you got your license (she trusted YOU—it was your friends she worried about), no skinny-dipping in the motel pool.

All the while Dr. Franky's pencil went SCRIBBLE TAP, SCRIBBLE TAP.

The 4th day, Daddy answered Q2. "Well, I did USE TO discipline Ash. Warmed his rear but good after I caught him & his friends playing Smokey the Bear, setting matches to a bush in the woods so they could stamp out forest fires. The bruises I left on him scared the hell outa me & Bonnie—I swore to her I'd never lay a hand on them kids again no matter what they done."

So that's what "Don't play with matches" meant.

"And I never did till Ash asked for it last summer—

he turned his brother's birthday party into an X-rated horror show. Anyways, I know God forgive me for disciplining him, cause the very day I started up to church the pastor had a message laid on him about not sparing the rod."

I remembered that one. How the Bible was the only child-rearing manual we'll ever need and no Christian should listen to Dr. Spock instead of the wise King Solomon. Who, by the way, didn't say "Spare the rod and spoil the child"—it was "He that spareth his rod hateth his son: but he that loveth him chastiseth him betimes." Pastor's eyes X-rayed Daddy. "So you parents, do you love your son, or do you hate him?"

That had scared me. Daddy'd been holding all that love into his belt buckle for so long, I was afraid he'd take the sermon to heart and show his feelings the next time I done something wrong.

Dr. Franky cleared his throat. "Ashton, what do you have to say?"

Shrug, "Hahaha."

Back to Dr. Franky. "Mr. Libby: Ashton has told me you—abused—him—frequently. Perhaps you will be able to recall other instances?"

PTOOEY! I couldn't believe that abuse cockamamy. As if little Ash didn't have a red rear coming, playing with fire! And that was the 1st I known of Daddy EVER spanking one of us kids, even though he probably felt like it plenty of times. I wanted to tell that doctor to go back to school.

Daddy says, "I did swat Ash's fanny the time he tried to plug his diaper pins into an electrical outlet. And another time he run out into the road when a truck was coming, scared the heck outa me. Went at him a few times to get the message through his diaper—could Ash be remembering THAT?"

"The first 2 or 3 years of life shape the child's psyche," says Frankenstein.

"Oh, Steve, how could we have brought such pain into the world?" snuffled Mama. Through her laryngitis. "I know it isn't Christian, but I don't think I can ever forgive myself."

"Come off it," says Deena. "Times like that it's IN-STINCT to swat a fanny—anyone who watches gorillas on public TV knows that. What you gonna do, stand there and say, 'Now sweetie pie, be a good little toddler and come out of the road so that naughty Mack truck don't think you're roadkill.'"

"There are nonviolent methods of discipline," says Frankenstein, and he started preaching what the psychology books laid on him.

I couldn't stand another second in that room. I jumped up. "I ain't setting here for no more of this TRIAL." And I went out to the car to wait.

The 5th day, which I'll never forget was February 28, I wanted to stay home. But Mama talked me into going back for your sake. To this day she wishes she didn't. Frankenstein asked Q4.

Dr. Finklestein as I Woulda Liked to Seen Him

"Can anybody recall instances of <u>incest</u> in the family?"

Well, while the rest of us was letting out 2 sets of shock sighs each—one cause he even asked & another one cause we'd have to mention the unmentionables in Deena's intervention letter—you finally decided to talk. You pointed right at Mama & Daddy and accused them of things even more disgusting than what you said about the Daigles, and it was all LIES.

Deena pointed her finger right at Dr. Franky and says, "I just decided what to give up for Lent," and walked out.

Your lies made me wish you'd never been born. But you was, so then I wished you'd hit another moose and it was the moose that lived.

Dr. Franky stopped scribble-tapping, looked hard into Mama & Daddy's hurt eyes, and says something sensible for once, "Is it not possible, Ashton, that on this particular point you are having trouble discriminating between <u>fantasy</u> and <u>reality</u>?"

Then I wished I hadn't wished you away. You're my brother. No matter what. It weren't your fault you was so sick. You wouldn't of brung out them hallucinations or whatever they was and called them memories, if Frankenstein hadn't asked for it.

Only one good thing about it—I figured something out. Daddy not sparing the rod on you when you was little musta made your whole idea of him different from mine. Now I could see what was behind you not telling on me & Merle the time we crossed the road when a truck was coming. The time you told Daddy you give me the blueberries I'd stole from Millard Worcester's field. The time you dug me & my boots out of the snow and didn't let on to the folks that I was jumping offen the roof. You thought you was saving me from the King Solomon side of Daddy's love.

Thank you, Ash.

March 7

That year was a leap year. An election year. An Olympic year. Years like that there's alot more losing going on than winning.

Did you win or lose February 29? The day after Q4.

Saved up your energy and got a good running start down the smoke ward hall so you could ram your head against the door. The only part of the wall that weren't padded. (It is now.)

According to what you told us on your suicide cassette (the hospital wouldn't give you nothing so sharp as a pen), the voices in your head made you do it. Told you what Sisyphus had to do in Hades weren't hell—pushing a rock uphill was LIFE. Told you to bust through that psych ward door to heaven, cause even if the rest of the human race weren't ready for God's digestion, God was ready for you.

The reason God wanted you on February 29, instead of some other day, was so our thoughts would leap right over the anniversary of your death every 3 out of 4 years.

There ain't no leaping over some thoughts—you oughta know that better than anyone.

You filled both sides of the tape with talk that didn't sound nothing like the guy who'd disgusted all 5 of our senses the day before. Like how much you loved having me, Deena & the folks as fellow raspberry seeds, and you was sorry if you said anything wrong about the family cause you was having a hard time telling what was real and what weren't. And how God told you life is a lived prayer that continues beyond death, and we wasn't suppose to look at your suicide as an act of despair but as an act of faith. We was suppose to smell the roses at your funeral and enjoy the music and pig out and live on.

But you didn't go to God like you wanted. Went into a coma.

The doctors said you might wake up any day, any month, any year, or never. But with modern technology hooked up to you, you could live forever in a coma. Okay, not forever, but it would seem it.

I hoped this crazy hope that you'd be like Jesus and rise up on the 3rd day of your coma. Or like that bird Miss Small's always harping on, the one in your song. The phoenix. It goes up in flames every 1000 years and is born again from the ASHes. More beautiful than ever. I hoped you'd be a phoenix, with all the voices erased and a new life ahead.

But the only part of you that was rising up was your lips in a yawn, and your eyeballs in a twitch under the lids. We was all excited at 1st, thinking this meant you was waking up, but the nurse said no, those little movements was common, "in the vegetative state." Well, I never seen no carrots or peas yawn and twitch. I known there was still a HUMAN BEING under your skin.

At this point you was in a different wing of the hospital. They was treating you comatose instead of crazy.

Somebody in the family went to visit you everyday to hold your hand and talk to you and basically try to "stimulate the patient's senses," like the doctor told us. Even though the day nurse kept saying, "He can't hear you—he's in a coma."

It made us cringe everytime the doctors pressed you and pinpricked you. But you didn't feel no pain.

Grammy Ethyl says, "Maybe he's better off this way, not hearing voices and making headlines," but she was just talking. I seen her squeezing your fingers and whispering sweet nothings in your ear just like the rest of us.

Krista come by—it surprised us. Her tears fell right on your face like they was your own, she wiped them off before she left.

Deena called you every ASH name in her vocabulary cause maybe it would piss you off enough to set up and bASH her one. But it didn't.

Mama brung in my breadbox. Maybe Hank Williams Jr. could wake you up. But the nurses didn't let us play the tape loud enough to get you in a dancing mood. Wouldn't wanna clash with their melodious Muzak.

Daddy shaved your stubble and slapped your cheeks with Old Spice and yelled, "Atten-HUT," among other commands. You didn't obey.

Pastor come to your bedside everyday on his way home from the factory and pled for stimulation from above: "Please God, reach down your merciful hand and raise Ash up out of this death-in-life so he too can live again, with You or with us, one way or the other, whatever Your will." There weren't no God hand coming down through the ceiling to tickle your ribs or snatch you away, though. And we was getting more than worried, we was desperate, cause with each day & week your chances of waking up was getting closer to slim or nil.

Around in there, Deena had to do her senior research paper for Miss Small. Deena had me read it to see if it made sense and to check for plagiarism since I had experience in that area. It was about depression, as if she had to do any research to find out what that was. Actually, her paper was excellent, even though she got a C minus for talking like Deena Libby instead of Dan Rather. My favorite part was, "Mental illness is like the common cold, everyone catches it sooner or later, but there's some who don't got the immune system to fight it off." She pointed out examples of how people who was "clinically depressed" described their horrors & gloom & dread just like the Bible describes hell, and some of them never even read the Bible. Which meant maybe religion was like a "metaphor" for the "psychological condition" of the writers.

See what you done to us, Ash? Before the moose, Deena would've writ her paper on Lowering the Drinking Age.

March 9

If anyone asked how you got in your coma—it was a freak thing, you hit your head. But truth squeezed into vague words got ways of spilling out (especially outa Deena). Every Sunday in March I expected Mrs. Fish-Lips to express her condolences to Mama & Daddy. "Sorry to hear Ash tried to kill hisself. Somebody up there must be watching out for him. No time to repent when your last sin's suicide."

Okay, maybe even she wouldn't of come out with such a crude comment, but she'd think it.

March 10

The scariest part of everything that happened after we hit the moose, is this. When I'm churning all your life in my head, there's moments when everything makes sense—the crazy things you said, and what you went and did to end it all.

What's the use of life, anyways?

Why bother?

Who cares? Just the few people who live around you, but they all die sooner or later too.

And then what difference does it make that you was ever here? Maybe it would matter if you could be like the people in the Bible and beget someone who begets someone really important. A Moses or a Gandhi or a Hank Williams Jr.

How many people do that?

How many people does the earth really need? There's too many people for one person to be important.

But most of the time, I know you was full of stink, Ash. You know damn well that the use of life is to LIVE. You're the one who saved my life twice. You're the one who blew up at Daddy for putting Togo to sleep. You're the one who ADMIRED the Upcountry Boys cause they kept at it even though they known it was useless wanting to be stars.

You musta forgot the bumper card you sent of your Nova.

> Life Is Fragile
> Handle with Prayer

On back you writ, "Offer each moment up to God by sucking life in through your ears, nose and throat."

Pastor & Daddy would disagree, but I know life on earth ain't just about preparing for the afterlife. Anyone with sense can see life is something in itself. A whiff of Mama's hair or a mouthful of Millard Worcester's blueberries or a violin playing real flashy's enough to

Well, I don't want to get sappy, it's just enough, that's all. And you use to know it.

March 11

*Life Is Fragile
I Better Write a Will*

March 12

The Bible guys was always calling themself ashes & dust. And back then they didn't even KNOW about microscopic man-eating sheep. There was so many ashes in Pastor's Easter sermon, I couldn't stop thinking of you.

Well, for a moment I thought of Merle's 2nd favorite Bible verse.

Ashes to ashes
And dust to dust,
All except for
Jeee-zus.

That Easter you was in your coma, Pastor skipped around explaining examples of how we'd be nothing but ashes in the furnace of hell if it wasn't for what Jesus done to make Easter a holiday. One example was Abraham before the big burnout at Sodom and Gomorrah: "Behold now, I have taken upon me to speak unto the Lord, which <u>am but</u> dust and ashes." Gen. 18:27—I remember cause I writ something in the margin.

The soul of Ashton
floats on dust—
behold him now
riding a
sunbe-
am.

March 13

I was getting wicked pissed. At the hospital for not waking you up even though they'd had 6 weeks to do it. At you for not waking up. At me for not having the power to change things.

I decided I weren't gonna set around waiting no more—I'd stay with you everyday of Easter vacation and try ANYTHING, no matter how dumb, to get the Ash breeze blowing again. When you're 100 points behind 1/2way through a Scrabble game, you jump at slim chances. It was like that.

"Hold on to your hat," I says.

I sneaked Mama's Easter-lily corsage out of the freezer—don't ask me why she bothers freezing flowers anyways since she just ends up throwing them out when she defrosts. And I held the lily under your nose.

I rubbed some of Grammy Ethyl's fudge on your tongue. And then squirted lemon on top so you'd REALLY want to spit.

I brung in a guitar string and pressed it into your fingers.

I taped myself playing violin in the bathroom. Doing the best I could with your Humpty-Dumpty squiggles. Trying my damndest not to scrape carrots. I bought a Walkman, loaded that cassette into it and held your hand while you "listened." (Told Mama it was Hank—she wished she'd thought of a Walkman sooner.)

I read you superhero comic books. Really POW-ing all the boldface and exclamation point words.

I told you knock-knocks and dirty limericks.

I says, "Let's go for a swim, Ash old boy," and flopped your arms & legs like so.

I lifted your lids and shined a flashlight in your eyes. While flashing your bumper-sticker postcards.

"Your move, cow," I says.

I done all these things and more, over and over and over. Mostly when nobody was looking. Why keep it a secret? I don't know—why do I keep Daddy's army medals on my G.I. Joe when everybody has to turn the house upside down looking for them every Memorial Day? Just had to, that's all. Like talking about it would jinx it.

Not to mention that Deena'd say, "Next time we're on the smoke ward Wes better check hisself in."

And you know what? This is gonna sound too unbelievable to happen in real life, and Daddy would say it was Jesus using me to answer prayers, but after I put you through the paces on the 3rd day of Easter vacation, you licked your lips & twitched your eyelids all the way open.

"I see I lived," you croaked. "How are Wes and the moose?"

March 14

Today you can smell spring in the mud.

When you get to the end of a book, you expect the end to be THE END, like some big problem's settled happily ever after. Only a couple pages left in the composition book, and still it ain't THE END. Even though I write small. I could scratch in another composition book

169

easy, except it would be hard. Besides, scratching this one took care of the itch. I feel 1000% better than I did January 1. Sleeping through the night, ain't had a headache since February, and I'm beating Deena to the 2nds. Like the stomach flu is over, and the next bite I eat will be the most delicious thing I ever tasted.

Now it's almost a year since you woke up from your coma, but you're still living unhappily ever after. The coma did clear your mind of lotsa memories after the moose, but you was still schizoid tended. You still got voices in your head, still got on-again off-again batteries. The doctors don't understand it at all, say it don't fit the pattern. Since when did Ashton Allen Libby fit the pattern?

There's been some high points. Like the country music company buying "Cloudy with a Chance of Pain," your old Wackos song, for someone like Randy Travis or Garth Brooks to make into a hit. Lately you been writing a lotta new songs I like—a guy could ask a girl to dance to them. Mama even suggested you perform entertainment at the 1st annual One Nation Under God party at church the 4th of July so everyone could boogie. Daddy said that was her Catholic showing—dancing ain't evangelical.

And you got your friends at the group home where you're living. They keep a good eye on you and don't let you bash your head into doors. Not that you won't end up doing yourself in by accident. When you was home this Christmas you tried to take a whole month's worth of medication in one dose. If one pill made the voices whisper in the back of your head instead of yell in your ears, then you figured a whole bottle oughta shut them up for good. It woulda, too, if I didn't walk in on you washing the pills down with a gallon of 2% milk. Finally got your stomach pumped after all.

Wish I had space to tell you how Merle & me started speaking again, when I went out to the Shibboleth on my big ONE FIVE, he was there. Instead of the sheet he'd hung down the middle to keep me offen his 1/2 all year, there was a life-size poster of a birthday cake with a hot pink redhead popping out of it.

I'm glad you didn't OD on purpose, Ash. You got reasons to breathe, so keep at it. A Knight of Sisyphus ain't a bad thing to be.

Forever your brother,
Wes

P.S. Okay, Merle, I take it back, I ain't gonna haunt you.
P.S. P.S. Merle, when you're telling your kids and grandkids what it was like growing up, I hope your best friend was me.